The Echo of Silence

A novel about Finding Home

BRENDAN T. KELLY

The Echo of Silence

A novel about Finding Home

BRENDAN T. KELLY

By Brendan T. Kelly
The Echo of Silence

DEDICATION

The Echo of Silence has been a heartfelt story to write, and honestly, a bit of therapy as well. I want to dedicate this book to all my brothers and sisters I've served with, and to those who still put on the uniform. I truly appreciate the sacrifices you've made and continue to make. To all those battling those negative internal demons and mental health challenges, I pray for you on your journey to find peace and acceptance. It takes guts and work to get to a place of comfort. To my dear friends, The Horsemen, you made life brighter when things got dark. For my mom, I miss you. Thank you for showing me what courage looks like. You never stopped fighting, and in the end, you won. To my lovely family and the best children a guy could have: your love, laughter, and spirit fill me with hope and a desire to do better. Then, to my soulmate, the love of my life, my amazing wife … thank you. Thank you for everything I have, for being there in my time of need, for your smile, and for your love.

PRAISE FOR
THE ECHO OF SILENCE

"*The Echo of Silence* moved me emotionally in ways I haven't experienced since my own recovery from military service. A powerful and deeply human story, *The Echo of Silence* captures the unseen battles that often follow long military service and war—the struggles, the fractures within, and the enduring search for peace. This is not just a war story—it is a story of survival, identity, and the long road toward healing. *The Echo of Silence* is an intimate journey that exposes harsh internal battles often fought in silence. Brendan T. Kelly weaves the past and present—from the chaos of the Iraq–Kuwait border to the quiet, stillness of civilian life—into a vivid, deeply personal narrative. *The Echo of Silence* resonates with authenticity and heart, and leaves readers with a lasting impact."
— CPT Kelly J. Galvin, USA (Ret), author of the screenplay, *PowerPoint Ranger*, based on his book, *PowerPoint Ranger: My Iraq War Logs*

"*The Echo of Silence* pulls back the curtain on what coming home really looks like, capturing both the physical and emotional toll of service. By painting a clear image of what coming back can look like and Jack's struggles with Post-traumatic stress and chronic health problems, I hope that other veterans will feel validated in their experiences and empowered to seek the help and support they need."
— Megan Falk, Military Writers Society of America Medalist, The SEAL Saga series

"Brendan T. Kelly hits an absolute homerun with his novel *The Echo of Silence*, an emotional roller coaster filled with the highs and lows of life spent in the service of others. From the opening pages of the book, I felt an instantaneous deep emotional connection with Jack Mercer. His experiences, personal vulnerability, and struggles he faces will resonate strongly with any soldier and their families that may be dealing with the uphill battle that warfighters face post-combat. For me, this was not just a story, and Jack Mercer was not just a character; it hit close to home. I commend Brendan for eloquently writing about topics that the veteran community far too often pushes into the shadows."
—SSG (R) Joe Troutman, author of *Gods of War: The Legend of Blackhawk Company 1/23 Infantry*

"In *The Echo of Silence*, Author Brendan Kelly has allowed Jack Mercer to be a window into his life. What we all see looking through Jack is Brendan's journey back from the abyss into a life of purpose."
— Travis Partington, Host of Oscar Mike Radio

1
A HAUNTED SOUL

The fog that rolled in overnight stayed well into the morning, thick and low, like a woolen blanket draped over the golden hills of Marin County. It clung to the redwoods and eucalyptus trees, quieting the world into a hush that felt almost angelic. In the distance the Golden Gate Bridge's foghorn sounded its slow, deep song, warning the vessels maneuvering around it. For most, it symbolized a peaceful start to the day. But for Jack Mercer, it was a reminder of what might have been.

He sat on the edge of the bed, elbows on knees, staring at the floor as if the carpet there might offer some form of motivation or at least tell him how he should get his day started. He stayed like that for some time, pondering, adrift, and then finally stood up slowly and stretched out toward the ceiling. The house was quiet. His wife, Elena, had already left for work. She always left quietly now, careful not to wake him. Or maybe she felt she was running out of things to say, tired of her words of encouragement fading away, seemingly unheard, into the stillness of the room. Jack couldn't blame her.

He rubbed his face with both hands, the stubble rough against his palms. Forty-seven years old, and 22 of those spent in the Army. His Army time had consisted of numerous duty stations, assignments, and deployments—three tours in Iraq, one in Afghanistan. His uniform had accumulated an array of medals that seemed pointless now, and he had a head full of ghosts that kept him company. To him, the ghosts made sense—not that he enjoyed them, but he knew why they were there. Jack had survived IEDs, ambushes, and the slow erosion of his own mind.

But civilian life? That had turned out to be the real war. Finding a place to fit in, a place that felt right. A place that provided purpose. He needed a purpose.

In the years since his retirement from the Army, he had yet to find a place that felt right. Had yet to find a real connection with others he worked with. Teaching high school had come close. But he had never truly bonded with the other teachers; they had been cliquish and gossipy. It was with his students he had felt a connection. He had understood the challenges they faced, the hardships of growing up in poor, single-parent families. Overall, they had been good kids. Just like many, they simply needed guidance and structure. He had been strict with them, but fair. He had treated them like adults and done his best to prepare them for life after high school.

He had taught for six years. It could have been longer, but he accepted a position with the Department of Labor. It had offered more money, no micromanaging parents to deal with, and it brought him and Elena back to Northern California, this time to the San Francisco Bay Area. To this day, he still received occasional text messages from students. Pictures of them and their families. Wedding notifications and even a few birth announcements.

The thought of his past students put a small smile on his face.

It was still early. He shuffled to the kitchen, his joints aching like rusted, oil-thirsty hinges. The coffee was already brewed—Elena's silent kindness. He poured a cup, black, and stepped out onto the back deck. The fog was thick today, swallowing the tops of the trees and the distant hills. Somewhere out in that murky grey air, the world moved along. Without him. Not needing him.

Jack took a sip and closed his eyes. The silence was almost too much. There was nothing serene about it. It was a static of nothingness. Only the occasional sip of coffee and his steady breathing broke the quiet. Far too often in the Army, silence meant danger. It meant something was coming. Goosebumps would run along his arms when he knew something was about to happen. A sixth sense. Now, it just meant he was alone with his thoughts.

And that was the problem.

He had tried to explain it, to Elena, to the VA therapist, to himself. The feeling of being untethered. Like a balloon cut loose from a child's hand, drifting higher and higher until the sky swallowed it whole. That's what retirement had felt like. Not freedom. Not peace. Just ... a disconcerting weightlessness. Still, a large part of him was happy to have retired. To have ended his part in a never-ending cycle of deployments. He was at peace with the decision.

The Army had given him structure, purpose, and a reason to get up every morning. But the price for that was nightmares, a jacked-up left shoulder, and a limp in his right leg, plus a list of names he couldn't bring himself to say out loud. But at least he'd known who he was.

Now? He wasn't sure.

The old Adirondack chair creaked beneath him, the wood weathered by the elements. The steam from his coffee curled upward in the cool air. He watched the fog slowly waltz over the hills and tried not to think about the pills in the bathroom cabinet or the Golden Gate Bridge, just a few miles away. A popular destination for so many, but for Jack, it held dark memories.

Thankfully, those were just passing thoughts now. He'd still find himself playing the story in his head, but he was able to push it away. It hadn't always been that way. He had given in to the darkness before.

PTSD, depression, and anxiety had haunted his soul and bled his life dry. Now, in the creaky chair, he thought of those memories. *They are a part of me. For better or for worse, until death do us part.*

As he got up and walked through the living room, he picked up a book he had been reading, *Creatures of the Day* by Irvin Yalom. He opened to a dog-eared page and read a line he had highlighted: "We must give up the hope for a better past." Those words had stopped his train of thought when he first read them. Seeing them again, he realized how much time he had spent hoping and wishing for things to not have happened, how much time he had spent fighting to change the past in his life and in his mind.

But of course the past had happened. It had left deep scars and painful memories.

All those damn memories.

2
DESERVING BETTER

Jack's first time had been at work, in a seldom-used storage room full of old furniture and dated recruiting pamphlets. The door was closed, pill bottle now empty. He'd sat there for what felt like an eternity, waiting for peaceful darkness to come. But it didn't. One of his soldiers, Sergeant Hart, had returned early from an appointment. For some unknown reason he had entered the storage room and found Jack, slumped over and making fragmented attempts to speak. He grabbed Jack and managed to get him into his car and to the small local hospital where the doctors and nurses pumped his stomach and gave him IVs.

Once he was stabilized and released, Jack and Sergeant Hart returned to the office in silence, only to have their unspoken thoughts greeted by the echo of the tick-tick from the wall clock. "Thank you," Jack said, finally finding words. He paused and took a deep breath. "I appreciate your help, and I am deeply sorry. I guess you can see I'm going through some shit?" he said, his defense mechanisms kicking in.

It took Sergeant Hart a few moments to get words out, and when he did, he sounded nervous. "I don't know what to do. I've never ..."

Jack interrupted him with a raised hand. "You don't have to do anything. But please keep this between us." He tilted his eyes down. "I know it's a big ask."

Sergeant Hart looked at Jack, serious and with concern in his eyes. "I think ... I think you need help."

"I do," Jack nodded. "I am going to get help. I promise. But I can't have this incident getting out."

Sergeant Hart's words were direct and filled with unease, but he relented. "I won't tell anyone. But you have to get some help."

That day was a dark cloud between them, an unsettling secret neither wanted to accept. Jack had not even considered he was dealing with Post Traumatic Stress Disorder, depression, and anxiety. He blamed his problems on his assignment with the United States Army Recruiting Command. The extreme hours, the never-ending mission of finding new recruits, and the chain of command that always demanded more, even when numbers were achieved.

Jack recalled a conversation with his First Sergeant right before Christmas. "You made mission, so now you're just going to quit on me and take it easy! I want two more fucking bodies in this month from your station!" he shouted and then hung up the phone.

Jack had sat in his office, attempting to control his anger. The control lasted one minute, then he grabbed the phone from his desk and threw it against the wall.

Those had been tough days and nights for Jack, and, despite his promises to Sergeant Hart, the Golden Gate was calling him. A second chance to finish the job. Elena would drop him off at the bus stop, as she did most mornings. He would get on the bus as usual, but he would exit at the bridge stop and end the madness once and for all.

Elena had recognized his dark mood that morning not long ago, cold and silent. She stopped the car and tried to reach him, but ... nothing. Jack looked down and began to cry. Then he began to yell. The 911 operator told Elena to get Jack to the nearest hospital immediately.

Jack broke through the mania three days later, waking up in the mental health wing of Marin General Hospital.

He was lucky to have a room to himself. No frills. A bed. A dresser attached to the wall. A bathroom with no door. A desk bolted to the floor, which sat in front of a frosted and barred window. The only thing he had control over, that he could move, was a wooden chair. He'd sit on it at night, legs propped on his bed, and read the books Elena had brought him.

A nurse had to buzz people in and out of the wing. The small outside courtyard was surrounded by a tall fence with barbed wire running along the top. Inside, endless rooms lined the corridors, some for sleep, others for meetings. Jack noticed a couple of them had padded walls. In the mornings and evenings, he walked laps around the inside, hands behind his back, observing everything and everyone around him.

The doctors prescribed Jack multiple medications, trying different strengths and combinations to help with anxiety, depression, and PTSD. Slowly, Jack's darkness began to lift. He asked questions during group sessions. He meditated in the mornings before breakfast. When the arts and crafts room was open, he drew and painted.

He spent two weeks in the hospital and another three months in an outpatient program. Elena and his family remained by his side, trying to help him find his way out of the darkness.

He had led men and women with strength and bravery, he had reached people and helped them learn, he had mentored people to believe in their efforts and in themselves. But for himself, all the advice felt hollow. It was incoherent. Made-up.

Yet, there was never a third attempt. Not because he didn't want to, but because he couldn't put Elena through that again. She deserved better. He finally accepted he deserved better.

But he wasn't whole. He felt fragmented, like shards of a man who once was something. But in those shards, he saw a reflection and, maybe, a moment of connection. *Aren't we all a little broken?*

3
THE STORM BREAKS

Jack drove into Mill Valley, a charming, artsy town nestled at the base of Mount Tamalpais, just off Highway 101. The road curved gently through groves of redwoods and eucalyptus, the air cool and fragrant with the scent of damp earth and salt carried in from the nearby bay. As he cruised into town, the trees gave way to narrow streets lined with ivy-covered cottages, boutique shops, and cafés with chalkboard menus and flower boxes spilling over with color.

Mill Valley was beautiful in a way that felt almost cruel—too perfect, like a postcard come to life. The kind of place where time seemed to slow down, where people walked their dogs with lattes in hand and children played freely in the park under the filtered light of towering trees. Sunlight dappled sidewalks, and breezes carried a faint sound of wind chimes and conversation. It was a kind of beauty that made Jack ache a little—not because it was unwelcome, but because it stirred something deep and nostalgic. A longing for simplicity. For peace. For something he couldn't quite name.

He parked near the town center and wandered. He didn't need anything; he just didn't want to be alone with his thoughts. He walked up the hill to the library, where he sat in the redwoods and listened to the creek. Beneath the massive redwood trees, the chilly air fell upon him. It was refreshing and helped wake his tired soul.

He made his way to the bookstore and lingered in the back, pretending to browse. The clerk gave him a polite nod but didn't approach him. Jack appreciated that. He wasn't in the mood for small talk.

Picking up a book on mindfulness, he flipped through a few pages and put it back. He didn't need a book to tell him how to breathe. He needed something real. Something that didn't feel like a Band-Aid on a bullet wound.

Outside, he sat on a bench and watched people pass. A young couple with a stroller. A man in cycling gear. A woman walking a golden retriever. They all looked so normal. Jack wondered if they ever felt like he did. Hollow. Disconnected. Like a ghost haunting his own life.

He reminded himself they certainly had their issues, too. His outpatient program had shown him that. He chuckled as he thought, *The only one that has it all together is the golden retriever.*

After a while he walked over to the market and grabbed a few things for dinner. He used to love to cook and had planned to go to culinary school after high school. But escaping the world he was stuck in back then was more important.

That evening, Elena got home later than usual. She looked tired. Her shirt was wrinkled, and her hair was pulled back in a loose bun. She smiled when she saw him in the kitchen chopping vegetables.

"You're cooking?" she asked, surprised.

"Trying something new," he said. "Figured I'd give you a break."

She kissed his cheek, soft and brief. "Thank you."

They ate in silence for a while. The clink of forks on plates filled the space between them.

"How was your day?" she asked eventually.

"Quiet," he said. "Went into town. I walked around."

She nodded. "That's good."

He wanted to tell her more. About the fog. The bookstore. The way he'd stared at the bridge on the long way home, thinking of what might have been. But the words stuck in his throat.

Instead, he said, "I've been thinking about going to some support group meetings, volunteering. Maybe at the county's VA center. Or with one of those veteran outreach groups."

Her eyes lit up a little. "That's a great idea, Jack."

"I don't know. Just thinking."

"Still. It's something."

He nodded. It was something. A start, maybe.

That night, he lay awake long after Elena had fallen asleep. The ceiling fan spun slowly above them, casting shadows that danced in silence across the walls. He listened to her breathing, steady and soft, and tried to match his own with it. He thought about the men he'd served with. The ones who didn't get home. The ones who did, but never really came back. He thought about the desert, the heat, the explosions in the distance. He thought about the silence that followed each engagement, how the barrage of artillery and gunfire would fill the air and then suddenly there would be nothing, an eerie moment of peace.

The never-ending nightmares, in all of their strange and horrifying presentations, were fading. It had been routine for Jack to wake in the middle of the night, drenched in a cold, heavy sweat, heart pounding like a drum in his chest.

The nightmare always began the same way—trapped in a small, windowless room, the walls closing in, the air thick and stale. From the shadows emerged grotesque clowns, their faces twisted into exaggerated grins, eyes wide and unblinking, their makeup smeared like war paint. They moved erratically, laughing in high-pitched, broken tones that echoed off the walls. Jack had no voice—he couldn't scream, couldn't call for help. All he had was a large machete in his hands, and the overwhelming instinct to fight. He swung wildly, desperately, trying to fend them off, but no matter how many he struck down, more kept coming. The room never emptied. The clowns never stopped. It was endless—chaotic, surreal, and terrifying. Only when he jolted awake, soaked in sweat and gasping for breath, did the nightmare release him. But even then, the images lingered, clinging to the edges of his mind like a spider's web.

Was it the new medications, or the process of time? Either way, the lessening of the nightmares was a relief. He still would wake up scared, unsure of where he was, unsure of what was real. He didn't know what tomorrow would bring, but for the first time in a long while, he didn't dread it. Tomorrow was no longer an enemy—not a friend, necessarily, but more of an ally. It would come. He would wake up. Get through the day. Eat. Then sleep.

Maybe for now, that was enough.

4
OPENING THE DOOR

Jack drove to the Marin County Veterans Center and stared at the glass doors like they might open on their own and pull him inside. The building was modest, grey, with a small American flag fluttering in the breeze. The Center was in a multipurpose building with other businesses: law firms, investment companies, and some county offices. A few cars were parked out front, most of them older models with faded bumper stickers: *Semper Fi, Army Strong, Support Our Troops,* and a few *Coexist.*

He hadn't opened these doors for over a year. The last time, shortly after he completed his outpatient program, he had attempted to sit through a group therapy session but left halfway through. Too many stories sounded like his own. Too many faces mirrored his pain. It had been too much. He wasn't ready.

It was more than just facing his vulnerability. Veterans Affairs had put a bad taste in his mouth after he retired. While he was working as a high school teacher, he had gone through the draining process of filing a VA claim. Even with all of his medical paperwork, military records, and written statements from people he served with, they treated him as if he was lying. As if he was trying to get one over on the government. It was a constant run-around. Appointment after appointment to confirm what they had already confirmed.

During his last appointment at the Dallas VA, Jack had sat stiffly in the worn pleather chair, arms crossed, jaw clenched. The VA psychologist across from him was young—too young, Jack thought—and her questions felt rehearsed, clinical, detached.

"How did that make you feel?" she asked, for the third time in 10 minutes.

Jack's patience finally snapped. "How the hell do you think it made me feel?" he barked, his voice rising. "I watched my friends die! I came home with pieces of them still in my head—their ghosts! And you're sitting there wanting to know if I felt 'sad' about it?" He stood up, pacing the room. "You don't believe me. You think I'm just another broken vet looking for sympathy. I don't need sympathy, I need someone who gets it." His hands were shaking.

The psychologist said nothing, just scribbled something in her notebook, and that made him even angrier. "Forget it," he muttered, grabbing his jacket. "You're not listening anyway."

He had stormed out of the office. Fed up and irritated with the bullshit he had to go through just to get help.

After his inpatient stay at Marin, he tried with the VA hospital in San Francisco. To his surprise, they were quick to respond and he had an appointment within a week. The VA rep was polite, helpful. He hadn't felt judged. "I have your records," she said. "I know what you've been through. I'm sorry for your past experiences. We'll take care of you here."

And they did. Within a couple of months, he received a disability rating from the VA. The disability pay was deposited into his checking account, and he even received a check for back pay from when he had first filed.

During his outpatient program, Jack had learned skills—slowly, deliberately—that helped him confront everything he had been through. And everything he was still going through. The days were structured but gentle, designed not to overwhelm but to guide. The group sessions were filled with people from all walks of life, each carrying their own invisible weight. Some struggled with crippling anxiety, others with depression that had hollowed them out. A few, like Jack, carried a tangled mix of trauma, grief, and the lingering effects of years spent in survival mode.

The counselors were calm, grounded, and deeply empathetic. They didn't try to fix anyone. They didn't tell Jack how he should feel or what he should do. Instead, they encouraged him to simply notice what he was feeling—to name it, sit with it, and understand it. Each morning began with a round-robin check-in: "How are you doing today?" No pressure to share, no judgement. Just space.

It was during these sessions that Jack was introduced to Cognitive Behavioral Therapy, or CBT. At first, it sounded clinical, almost too structured for the mess he felt inside. But as the days went on, he began to see its power. CBT didn't ask him to forget what he'd been through—it helped him reframe it. He learned how thoughts could shape emotions and how emotions could drive behaviors. He began to recognize patterns: the way a single negative thought could spiral into a full-blown panic, or how guilt from the past could cloud his ability to enjoy the present.

One exercise stuck with him. The counselor had asked them to write down a recurring negative thought and then challenge it—like a lawyer cross-examining a witness. Jack wrote: "I'm a failure." It was this thought that berated him on days he couldn't get out of bed, when his thoughts whirled on not being selected for senior level promotions, on giving up on life. Through CBT, he learned to ask: "Is that true? What evidence do I have? What would I say to a friend who said this about themselves?" Slowly, he began to dismantle the belief, piece by piece.

CBT gave Jack tools—not just to cope, but to reclaim control. He started journaling, tracking his moods, identifying triggers. He practiced grounding techniques when anxiety crept in and used breathing exercises before a new storm took control. It wasn't a miracle cure, but it was a foundation. Something solid to stand on.

Perhaps most importantly, it reminded him that healing wasn't about erasing the past. It was about learning to live with it—and still move forward.

As Jack opened the doors to the Veterans Center, he was cautious. He always had his guard up, scanning every room for exits, reading faces for the slightest shift in tone or expression. It wasn't just awareness—it was hypervigilance, a constant, exhausting readiness for danger that never seemed to fade. But something had shifted. Maybe it was Elena's tired smile. Maybe it was the way the fog had lifted just a little faster that morning.

He stepped inside.

The air smelled faintly of coffee and disinfectants, a sterile warmth that clung to the muted walls and scuffed floor. The soft hum of fluorescent lights buzzed overhead, with one flickering in and out, blending with the distant clatter of an overworked printer. Behind a layer of glass and an unorganized desk, a receptionist looked up, her fingers pausing mid-keystroke. She offered a courteous, practiced smile. Her eyes flicked briefly over Jack, assessing, welcoming, and ready to move on to more pressing matters. "Good morning," she said. "Can I help you?"

Jack hesitated. "I'm ... thinking about volunteering. Maybe helping out with outreach or peer support."

Her smile widened. "That's great to hear. We're always looking for vets who want to give back. Let me get someone from the program office."

She disappeared down a hallway, and Jack stood awkwardly in the lobby, hands in his pockets. A few other veterans sat in the waiting area, an older man with a cane, a woman in her thirties scrolling through her phone, a young guy with a service dog curled at his feet. No one looked at him. No one needed to.

A few minutes later, a man in a flannel shirt and jeans approached. He was in his fifties, with a thick grey beard and kind eyes.

"Jack Mercer?" he asked, extending a hand.

"Yes."

"I'm Tom. I run the peer support program here. You served?"

"Twenty-two years. Army."

"That's a hell of a run. Come on back. Let's talk."

Tom led him to a small office with mismatched chairs and a whiteboard covered in sticky notes. The two men sat down across from each other. Tom listened more than he spoke. Jack appreciated it.

"I've been out for a few years. I tried a few things. Nothing stuck. I've got ... stuff I'm still working through. But I thought maybe helping other guys might help me, too."

Tom leaned back in his chair. "That's usually how it starts. You think you're doing it for them, but it ends up being just as helpful for you, too."

Jack looked down at his hands. "I don't know if I'm ready. It's hard to hear the stories. I don't even like hearing mine."

"Becoming ready can be a long wait. But you showed up today. That's a first step, and more than most take."

They talked for nearly an hour. Jack was appreciative of Tom's time. He felt like Tom had other things to do, but Tom gave Jack the time he needed. By the end, Jack had agreed to sit in on a peer group the following week. Just observe. No pressure.

As he left the building, something strange stirred in his chest. Not hope, exactly. But maybe the memory of it?

That night, Elena noticed. "You seem lighter," she said as they sat on the couch, a movie playing quietly in the background.

"I went to the county VA center. I talked to a guy about volunteering."

She turned to him, eyes wide. "Really?"

He nodded. "I'm going to check out a group next week. Just to see."

She reached for his hand and squeezed it. "I'm proud of you."

He didn't know what to say to that, so he just held her hand and let the silence settle around them—not so heavy this time, and a little warm. Like a blanket instead of a burden.

The days that followed were still hard. The nightmares still came. The mornings still felt like climbing out of a pit. But there was a thread to hold onto now. A line connecting him to something outside himself.

He started going for longer walks around his neighborhood. Appreciating the world around him. Talking more. He even called an old Army buddy he hadn't spoken to in years. They talked for two hours, mostly about nothing. But it felt good.

The fog still came, but it didn't stay as long.

And when he stood on the deck in the early morning light, coffee in hand, he didn't think about the bridge. He thought about Elena, their three amazing daughters, and the group he'd meet with later that day. The stories he might hear. The ones he might share.

He wasn't healed. Not even close.

But he wasn't completely adrift anymore.

He was trying to find his way back. Back to something resembling life. Whatever that looked like.

5
DUST AND DREAMS

Wellington, Texas, 1980

Like many small towns across the country, Wellington had a small square, made up of shops surrounding an old courthouse. A surprisingly big and ornate post office. A couple small grocery stores. A Sears catalog store. One clothing store. A movie theater that had been under renovation for years. One elementary school. One middle school. One high school. Population just under 5,000 people. Wellington also had a steel mill and a couple cotton gins. There was a Dairy Queen and two Allsups convenience stores, one on the north side of town and the other by the high school.

In Wellington, you were either a farmer, rancher, steel worker, cotton processor, shop owner, or married to someone with one of those jobs. The other occupation, though unpaid, was being a town gossip. In fact, gossiping was a requirement. It was an effective way of getting the news—much better than relying on the small local newspaper or any of the news channels. Little old ladies were professionals at translating daily life into juicy, elaborate tales of mischief. And the men had their own version of gossiping. It was closer to the truth, and made better with their explicit language.

The summer heat in Wellington didn't just sit on your skin, it penetrated your bones. It was the kind of heat that made the air shimmer above the asphalt and turned the dirt roads into powder. Jack Mercer was 10 years old that summer, and, for his part, he didn't care one bit about the heat. He had a pair of scuffed-up boots, a straw hat a size too big, and some serious dreams.

He wanted to be a bronc rider. Not just any bronc rider, but a world champion. A champion they talked about on the radio and wrote about in *Rodeo Sports News.* He loved a good rodeo. The sights, sounds, and the atmosphere were electric. His grandma had taken him to the Tri-State Fair and Rodeo in Amarillo last September. Jack loved the food, but, unlike the other children, he didn't care much for the rides. He was focused on seeing the rodeo. Men with sun-leathered faces and quiet eyes, walking like they carried the weight of something invisible. Jack had watched them ride like they were born in the saddle, and something inside him had ignited.

That summer, he spent every spare minute at the rodeo grounds on the edge of town. It wasn't much, just a few rusted gates, a dusty arena, and a couple of old practice dummies made from barrels and rope. But to Jack, it was sacred ground.

During his childhood, that place of dirt with its weathered fencing and tight chutes became a sanctuary. He could easily escape life as soon as his feet stepped into the arena.

With each new visit or extended stay at his grandma's place, he found his way to the rodeo grounds in Wellington. It was there he felt alive. He rode steers and young broncs and had ideas of turning his dreams into something more.

He'd climb the fence and sit on the top rail, watching the ropers practice. Sometimes they let him help, holding the gate, fetching gear, brushing down the horses. He didn't mind the humble work at all. Every second out there was a lesson.

There were days Jack and his friend Doug would show up to the rodeo grounds in the morning and spend all day there. Sometimes they would ride steers that the local ranchers brought in for branding or shots. Other times they ran down calves and tried to wrestle them to the ground. Jack rode his first bronc, staying on for just shy of six seconds. As fast as that ride went by, it lived on for months in his mind.

Every so often, a rancher would ask for Jack and Doug's help, saying, "Boys, I'll get each of you a soda if you can put those calves into pen number three."

With a nod, Jack and Doug would go after the calves, flanking them and moving towards the pin. Jack would run up and open the gate, using it to guide the calves. Then, when all the calves had entered, he and Doug would move in fast and close the gate, each one looking at the other as if they had won a genuine rodeo title.

"Job well done, cowboys. Come get yourself a cold one," the rancher would say. The ranchers were always kind and appreciative of their help.

Even when Jack and Doug were attempting to ride their steers, the ranchers just watched and laughed. Jack figured it brought back memories from their youthful days. And they knew a couple scrawny little boys weren't going to do any damage to their herds.

Jack lived with his step-grandma, Treva Mercer, on the edge of town, in a small white house that had peeling paint and a porch swing that creaked in the wind. She was a tough woman, wiry and sharp-tongued, with a cigarette always burning and a Bible perpetually nearby. She'd raised three kids of her own, and now, somehow, had found the strength to do it again.

Jack's mom, Carla, was constantly battling addiction, piecing together a string of sober months here and there, appearing to be winning, but then once again taking a turn for the worse. She struggled to provide Jack and his siblings even the most basic necessities. Food was scarce, clothes were hand-me-downs, and the comfort and security of consistency was rare. Yet, amidst the chaos and hardship, Jack's spirit remained unbroken. He possessed a fierce, almost defiant will to find joy in the small things—like the beauty in a sunset over the plains of the Panhandle or the sweet taste of a freshly picked tomato from his grandma's garden.

His mother's struggles were not a secret to most of the family, nor to many folks around town. However, whether due to youthful ignorance or a naturally joyful outlook on life, Jack didn't notice it or didn't want to believe it. The hushed tones of concerned neighbors, the stealthy glances exchanged across the street, and the ever-present anxiety etched on his mother's face were just part of Jack's life as he knew it. His older sister and brother understood, and they carried the emotional burden.

His mom was in and out of rehab but mostly out. She'd show up after a spell, feeling better, temporarily, promising to all that she was clean for good and ready to be a mother again. His dad? He was just a name on a birth certificate. Not much talk about him. The occasional call between him and Carla was always an argument, and short-lived.

Grandma Treva didn't coddle. She believed in chores, early mornings, and telling the truth even when it hurt (unless she was gossiping about what might be happening around town). She loved Jack fiercely, in her own way. She made sure he had clean clothes, hot meals, and a roof over his head. And when he came home with scraped knees and wild stories from the rodeo grounds, she'd just shake her head and say, "You're going to break your fool neck one of these days."

"Not before I win the buckle," he'd say, grinning.

Before she even let him step foot in the house, she'd demand he strip down and then she'd rinse him off with the hose.

One evening, Jack sat out back by the garden, his boots dusty and his shirt stuck to his back with sweat. Grandma Treva brought him a glass of sweet tea and sat beside him, lighting a cigarette with a practiced flick of the lighter.

"You been out there all day?" she asked.

"Yes ma'am."

"You eat anything?"

"Had a double-decker bologna sandwich."

She nodded, exhaling smoke. "You really think you're going to be a bronc rider?"

"I know I am."

She looked at him for a long moment, her eyes softening. "It's a hard life, Jack. Harder than you know."

"I ain't scared."

"That's what scares me."

They sat in silence for a while, the cicadas buzzing in the trees. Jack watched the sun dip below the red dirt fields, painting the sky in streaks of orange and purple. He felt something swell in his chest, something like hope, or maybe just the certainty that he was meant for more than this dusty little town.

That summer, he built his own practice rig in the backyard. An old oil drum strapped between two sawhorses, with an old saddle and a rope for reins. He'd ride it for hours, pretending the crowd was cheering, pretending he was holding on for those eight seconds that felt like forever. Sometimes, when the wind was just right, he could almost hear the announcer calling his name: *"Jack Mercer, from Wellington, Texas! Let's see what this young cowboy's got!"*

And in those moments, he wasn't the kid with a broken family and a mama who couldn't stay clean. He was a champion. A rider. Somebody.

But dreams, like horses, have a way of bucking you off when you least expect it.

One afternoon in late August, Jack came home to find his mom sitting on the steps to the back porch, her arms wrapped around her knees. She looked thinner than he remembered, her eyes sunken and her hands shaking.

"Hey, baby," she said, her voice barely above a whisper.

He froze. "What are you doing here? Are you done working out of town?"

"I came to see you. I know I've been out of touch for too long."

Grandma Treva stood in the doorway, arms crossed, her face like stone. "She's only here for a bit today," she said.

"I need to share something with Jack," Carla said quietly. "Please."

Jack didn't know what to feel. Part of him wanted to run to her and just be thankful his mom was back home. But the unsure part made him just stand there, waiting for what she had to share.

"I'm getting married, baby." Carla's words come across shaky.

Jack was in shock. Questions ran through his head. The only one he could get out was perhaps the most important. "Are we staying here, though?" he asked.

Silence filled the air for the better part of a minute. In the silence, Jack knew the answer.

Carla was still holding her knees, and her words were filled with minimal hope. "We have to move back to California, baby," she said. "It's where Gary works."

Over dinner, Jack thought of how he could kindly ask to stay here. This was his home now. He couldn't leave.

"What if I stay here and help out Grandma?" he finally asked.

He could see his grandma's eyes softening. His mom picked at her food, talked about getting a job back in Sacramento, about maybe getting a place where Jack could have a big yard. Jack understood the unspoken answer. He didn't say much else throughout dinner. Just nodded and stared at his plate.

That night, his mother left. Jack watched her walk out to the road and get in her car and drive away, the car's red taillights slowing fading into the darkness.

He laid in his bed and stared out the window for what felt like hours. The sky was clear, and a soft breeze found its way through his window, carrying the scent of freshly plowed fields. He thought about the rodeo grounds. His playground. He had some wonderful memories to carry with him. The setting sun that filled the sky with vibrant colors had faded to deep indigo, with a sliver of pale crimson light off on the distant horizon. To most, this was just a flat, easy to forget landscape. A place you flew over or quickly drove through. To Jack it was freedom. Freedom to be himself. To have big dreams.

A few weeks later, he was packed up and sitting in the back seat of an old dark green Ford four-door. He felt helpless. His grandma stood on the front lawn and watched them drive away. As they passed the rodeo grounds, Jack had the urge to jump from the car and run. Run to the only home he really knew.

With his new stepdad, Gary, driving, and his mom in the passenger seat, Jack stared through the large back window. He watched the rodeo grounds and Wellington fade away as they got further down Highway 83. His forehead pressed against the back window, Jack watched as the flat plains of the Texas Panhandle stretched endlessly into the horizon. The sun was just beginning to rise, casting long shadows across cotton fields and rusted windmills. His mom sat quietly, her hands folded in her lap. His stepdad drove with one hand on the wheel, his other resting on the open window, fingers tapping to the rhythm of a country song playing low on the radio.

As they crossed into New Mexico on I-40, the landscape began to shift. Flatness gave way to mesas and scrubland, then to the dusty reds and oranges of New Mexico. Jack watched it all pass by as if in a movie—abandoned gas stations, roadside diners, freight trains crawling along distant tracks. He didn't say much. He just watched. Somewhere near Flagstaff, Arizona, he saw snow on the high, craggy mountains. By the time they crossed into California, the desert had taken over, then that too disappeared and turned to orchards and vineyards, and the air began to change. It felt heavier, like something new and unknown was waiting. Sacramento was still hours away, but Jack already felt the distance growing between who he had been and who he might become.

Years later, Jack would learn the truth about his mother's addiction. The knowledge came not like a thunderclap, but like a slow, creeping fog settling into the corners of his memory, reshaping his past in quiet, painful ways. He felt naive at first, almost foolish. How could he not have seen it? The signs were there, weren't they? The long absences, the sudden mood swings, the way she sometimes stared through him like he was a ghost.

But then he'd remind himself, he had been just a kid. A boy with calloused palms and wild dreams of becoming a world champion bronc rider. His world had been made of dust and sunlight, of horses that kicked like lightning and the sound of his grandma's voice calling him in for supper. He hadn't been looking for cracks in the foundation. He'd been too busy building castles in the clouds.

In the quiet moments, those fragile spaces between nightmares and memories, Jack would drift back to that summer. The one that lived in his bones like a song he couldn't forget. He'd think about the rodeo grounds, how they shimmered in the heat like something out of a dream. He remembered the smells of sweat, leather, hay, and something else he could never quite name. Something sacred. Like the earth itself was holding its breath, waiting for the next bronc ride.

He'd remember the way his grandma's hands felt, weathered and warm, as they ruffled his hair, her voice steady and sure as she told him he was stronger than he knew. Back then, he believed her. Back then, strength meant holding on tight and not letting go, even when the world bucked and twisted beneath you.

He never became a bronc rider. Life, as it often does, had other plans.

Plans that didn't involve arenas or trophies or the roar of a crowd. But sometimes, when the day was long and his mind wandered, he'd find himself back there. In the dust. In the dream.

He could smell the dirt, feel it cling to his boots. He could hear the snort of a restless horse, the creak of saddle leather, the distant call of his name. And for a fleeting moment, he was 10 years old again, bareback on a wild horse, heart pounding, eyes wide with wonder. Riding like the world hadn't yet taught him how to fall.

6
THE CIRCLE

The first thing Jack noticed when he walked into the veteran's meeting room was the silence. Not the absence of sound, exactly. There was a faint hum of fluorescent lights, an occasional clink of a coffee mug, a shuffle of feet on linoleum. But a deeper kind of silence. The kind that came from people who had seen too much and learned to say too little about it.

The room was stark, with white walls and a flyer-crowded bulletin board near the door. Windows on the wall let in the morning light. A circle of fiberglass chairs, colors faded and legs carrying the weight of more than the people in them, centered the room. No tables. No podium. Just chairs. Equal footing. No rank here.

Jack hesitated in the doorway, his hands still on the frame. He could turn around. No one would stop him. No one would even know he'd come. He could leave and get in his car and take a drive through the countryside. Maybe go to the beach and just sit.

But he stepped in.

Tom looked up from the coffee pot and smiled. "Jack," he said. "Glad you made it. Grab a seat."

Jack nodded and took a chair near the wall, so he could see the door and room around him. He sat stiffly, his back straight, hands resting on his thighs. The others were already there. Eight of them, maybe nine. Men and women. Different ages, different branches. All of them carried something in their eyes that Jack recognized. The pain of past events and ghosts that never moved on.

Tom clapped his hands once. "Alright, let's get started."

Briefly the silent room became very still.

"Welcome back, everyone. And welcome to Jack, first time joining us. No pressure to share today, just listen if that's what you need."

Jack gave a small nod. He didn't like being called out. It felt strange. All of this felt strange. A few others nodded back at Jack. No lingering stares. No one asked questions. That was something.

Tom continued. "Let's do what we always do. Speak your truth. No judgement. No fixing. Just listening."

There was a pause. The kind that stretches just long enough to make the silence feel heavy. Then Ray spoke.

He was in his late forties, Army vet, with a buzz cut that had grown out unevenly, like he'd stopped caring halfway through. His face looked like it had been carved from stone, with sharp lines, deep creases, the kind of weathered look that told you he'd seen things most people couldn't even imagine. His eyes were tired, but alert, like they were always scanning for something just out of sight.

"I had a bad one this week," he said, voice low and gravelly. "Woke up screaming."

He paused and took a deep breath.

"My wife doesn't even flinch anymore. She just rolled over and went back to sleep." He let out a bitter chuckle. "That's how normal it's become."

He looked around the circle, his gaze landing briefly on each person. "I hate that," he said. "I hate that she's used to it."

No one jumped in. No one offered advice or tried to soften the moment. That was the rule here: no fixing, just listening. Just holding space.

Ray shifted in his seat, the old chair creaking beneath him. "In the beginning," he continued, "she'd sit up with me. Hold my hand. Ask me what I saw, what it meant. She tried to understand it, tried to make sense of why I was waking up drenched in sweat, heart pounding like I'd just run a marathon."

He rubbed the back of his neck, eyes distant. "But after a while ... I guess it became too much. Too heavy. She stopped asking. Stopped trying to fix it. And I stopped trying to explain."

The room was still. A stillness that blends into a silence of understanding and empathy.

Ray spoke for a while longer. Not in a rush, not looking for pity. Just laying it out, piece by piece. His voice didn't waver. There was no drama in it, just truth. Raw and unfiltered. And somehow, that made it comforting. Not because it made anything better, but because it reminded everyone in that circle they weren't alone. That someone else had been there, too. Was still there.

Next was Denise. She sat with her arms crossed tightly over her chest, like she was holding something in. The faded Marine Corps tattoo on her upper arm peeked out from beneath the sleeve of her T-shirt—an eagle, globe, and anchor inked in black and red, the edges softened by time and sun. Her jaw was set, her posture rigid, like she was bracing for an impact.

"I went to a school this week," she said, her voice steady but low. "Talked to a bunch of high schoolers about military service. You know, the usual—discipline, opportunity, teamwork."

She paused, her eyes scanning the floor like she was replaying the moment in her head. "One of them asked me if I ever killed anyone."

The words hung in the air like smoke. No one moved. Her jaw tightened. She took a breath through her nose, slow and deliberate.

"I told him the truth. I said, 'I don't know. I patched up people who didn't make it. I called in medevacs that never landed. I held pressure on wounds that wouldn't stop bleeding. You tell me."

She looked down at her hands, turning them over slowly, as if expecting to still see blood there. "It just came out. I didn't plan to say it like that. But it kind of felt good. Like I stopped pretending for a second."

There was a long silence. Not uncomfortable, just respectful. Everyone in the room knew what it meant to carry something you couldn't explain. To be asked questions that had no clean answers.

"I'm tired of acting," she said finally, her voice quieter now. "Tired of giving the polished version. The one that makes people feel better. As a recruiter, I want to tell the truth to these kids, no bullshit like I was fed."

She gave a small, dry laugh. "On a positive note, the kid didn't ask any more questions."

A few people in the circle smiled—not out of amusement, but recognition. That kind of moment, that kind of honesty, was rare. And it mattered.

Denise didn't say anything else. She didn't need to.

Carlos, a former Navy SEAL, spoke next. He was quiet, almost shy, the kind of man who didn't waste words. But when he did speak, the atmosphere in the room shifted. People leaned in, not out of politeness, but because they knew whatever he said would be impactful.

"I went to the mall with my daughter," he began, his voice soft, almost hesitant. "First time in years."

He paused, rubbing his palms together slowly, like he was trying to warm them or ground himself.

"She wanted to go to the food court. Kept talking about those soft pretzels she likes. I said okay. Figured I could handle it."

He looked down, a faint smile tugging at the corner of his mouth. "We were walking past the escalators. It was loud, kids yelling, music playing from some kiosk. I was on edge, but I was holding it together."

Then his expression shifted, the smile fading. "Someone dropped a tray. Big metal one. Loud crash. Echoed off the tile like a gunshot."

He stopped, eyes distant now.

"I didn't think. I just ducked down and grabbed my daughter. Pulled her close, shielded her. Just like that. Like I was back over there."

He shook his head slowly, as if trying to dislodge the memory.

"She didn't cry. Didn't scream. She just ... kneeled next to me. Put her little hand on mine. Didn't say a word. Just stayed there until I could breathe again."

His voice cracked slightly, and he blinked hard, trying to clear the glassiness from his eyes.

"She's eight," he said. "Eight years old. And I know she has some idea of what I've been through. She's seen the way I flinch at fireworks, the way I check every exit when we walk into a room."

He looked up, meeting the eyes of the others in the circle.

"But I should be the strong one."

There was a long silence. Full of understanding, of shared weight. No one needed to say anything. They all knew what it meant to be caught between the past and the present, between who you were and who you were trying to be for the people you love.

Malik, the youngest in the group, wore a hoodie pulled low over his face. He spoke without looking up.

"I don't sleep. I don't eat. I don't talk to my mom. I don't answer my phone. I don't know why I'm here."

He paused.

"But I came back. That's something, right?"

Tom nodded. "That's everything."

Frank, the Vietnam vet, leaned forward in his chair. His voice was slow, deliberate.

"I've been coming here for 10 years. I still have dreams about the jungle. I still wake up thinking I'm 20 years old and covered in leeches. But I come here because this is the only place where I don't have to explain myself."

He looked at Malik and turned and looked at Jack.

"You'll see. It helps."

Jack felt the weight of their stories settle on his shoulders. Not as a burden, but as a kind of invitation. These people weren't just surviving. They were showing up. They were speaking the unspeakable. He thought about the years he'd spent in silence. The angry moments and inability to release the rage within, nights staring futilely at the ceiling. The mornings he didn't want to wake up. The pills. The bridge. This damn life.

He thought about Elena's quiet strength. About the way she still looked at him like he was worth saving. And then, without planning to, he spoke.

"My name's Jack," he said. His voice sounded foreign in his own ears. "Army. Twenty-two years. Retired in 2010."

He paused. The room was still.

"I've been to a lot of places I wish I hadn't. Seen things I can't forget. Lost people I can't stop thinking about. Did things that are engraved in my memory."

He looked at his hands, lightly shaking, then back up.

"I tried to end it. Twice. Once when I was still in service and then afterwards. I don't remember much after my second attempt, except for waking up in a mental health unit with my wife beside me. Both times, I was angry I was still here."

He swallowed hard. Small beads of sweat formed on his forehead.

"I don't know who I am in this life anymore. I knew when I was in uniform. I don't know how to be a husband, or a friend, or even a person some days. I feel like I'm floating. Like I'm not real."

He looked around the circle. People nodding, some with looks of understanding.

"But seeing and hearing some of you ... it's the first time I've felt like maybe I'm not alone in this. That it's not just me. Maybe I don't have to carry it all by myself."

He exhaled, long and slow. He fought back tears, still finding it a challenge to be vulnerable.

"I can't live like this anymore, and I want to live. I don't know how yet. But I want to try."

The silence that followed wasn't empty. It was heavy with respect and understanding.

Tom nodded. "Thank you, Jack. That took courage."

Ray leaned forward. "You're not floating anymore, brother. You're here. With us."

Denise added, "You're one of us now. Whether you like it or not."

There were small smiles. Not forced. Not pitying. Just real.

After the meeting, Jack lingered. Malik came up to him.

"Hey," he said. "What you said ... that hit me. I feel that way, too. Like I'm not real."

Jack nodded. "You are definitely real. Otherwise, I'm seeing things." There was a gentle laugh.

Malik looked down, then back up. "Are you coming next week?"

"Yeah, I'm going to try," Jack said. "I find myself taking things one day at a time."

That night, Jack sat on the back deck, the stars bright above the Marin hills, the sonorous foghorn soothing in the distance. Elena came out and sat beside him, her hand finding his.

"How was it?" she asked.

He looked at her, really looked at her.

"It was hard," he said. "But good. I talked. I listened. I didn't feel alone."

She smiled, tears in her eyes.

"I'm proud of you," she murmured.

He squeezed her hand. "For the first time in a long time," he said, "I felt understood, in a shared understanding kind of way. Not judged. I could just be. There was no crap about, 'You're loved. You have value in this world.' Just people listening and understanding."

Elena was hopeful. She also acknowledged there would continue to be peaks and valleys. After all, he still had work to do.

Jack knew this, too.

7

THE FIRST SILENCE

Iraq–Kuwait Border. February 24, 1991

They had arrived in Saudi Arabia almost three months ago. Time was spent preparing their equipment. Waiting on ships to arrive with their vehicles. Picking up supplies at the airbase. Each day was a step toward the inevitable. Senior leaders talked a good game about how the situation could still end in a peaceful resolution. Inside, Jack knew better. As did others. Peace was no longer an option. Not with the amount of firepower arriving every hour.

Generals talked about how the Air Force had practically wiped out Saddam's military. *Then why do they need us?* Jack would think. His platoon kept preparing. New meetings with other units each day. Discussing strategies. Formations. The use of deadly force. Then one day they were told to load all their equipment on the vehicles. "Get your needed supplies. We roll out tonight to a forward staging position near the border."

The drive was long. Multiple stops to refuel, eat, and rest for a brief 15 minutes. Finally they halted. They were ordered not to set up tents or any other structures and were told to be prepared to move at any moment. They stayed in that spot for a week and then were finally instructed to prepare their vehicles for combat. "Tie everything down you won't need. Upload your weapons. We move out at 0400."

The desert was a void, the sky black from burning oil wells, windless and endless. Jack sat in the turret of an M113 track vehicle – an M16 rifle cradled in his lap, a 50 caliber rifle in front of him. The weapon was locked and loaded, his body fully armored, and his mind raw and exposed. The only light came from the red glow of the instrument panel and the occasional flicker of tracer fire in the distance. The invasion had begun.

The night before, he had stood just outside the perimeter of the forward staging area, the desert air cool and still, and watched as the horizon lit up in flashes of roaring artillery fire. A battery of howitzers, hidden in the darkness, unleashed volley after volley into the distance, each blast echoing with a deep, resounding concussion that rolled across the sand like thunder. The sky flared with fiery pulses of orange and white that lit up the low clouds. A display of raw power, a calculated tempest meant to soften enemy positions before armored division moved in. Jack watched it all in silence, the ground trembling beneath his boots, knowing this was only the beginning. It was awe-inspiring and terrifying.

He was 21 years old. A private first class. At times he felt like that kid from Wellington, Texas, who used to ride barrels made from oil drums and dreamed of rodeo glory. Now, he was part of the 1st Infantry Division, rolling into Iraq under the cover of darkness, part of a massive armored push that would become one of the fastest ground campaigns in modern warfare.

But no one had told him how loud it would be, even through his headset. The noise was overpowering, beyond imagination.

The vehicle roared forward, its treads grinding over sand and rock. The air inside was thick with the rank smells of sweat and anticipation. Jack's team leader, Sergeant Donel, was taking his turn driving, acting as calm as ever, chewing gum like they were just on another training op.

"Keep your head down, Mercer," he said. "And don't freeze up."

Jack replied over the intercom. "Roger," he said, his jaw clenched. He could feel his heartbeat in his throat.

The radio crackled. "Contact front. Bunker position. Two hundred meters. Return fire authorized."

The desert exploded.

One after another, the M1 Abrams tanks opened fire, each tank with their 120mm smoothbore cannons sending round after round at their targets. The recoil shook the earth, and the sound was deafening—a deep, chest-pounding boom that echoed for miles. Dust and smoke billowed around the tanks with each shot, and Jack could feel the shockwaves rippling through his chest. It was truly a symphony of destruction, relentless and annihilatory. In that moment, the battlefield felt like a living thing. Angry, loud, and utterly unstoppable.

Jack scanned the area in front of the M113, his heart pounding. The world was chaos now, awash with shouts over the radio, gunfire, the thump of mortars, and tanks firing. An Iraqi bunker was dug into a low ridge, about 100 yards away, barely visible in the dark. Muzzle flashes from the bunker blinked like fireflies. Bullets snapped through the air overhead.

He aligned the .50 cal and fired multiple bursts, the recoil jolting his body violently. He fired again. And again. Training took over.

"Hold your fire! Hold your fire! I'm falling in behind the M1 at three o'clock!" Donel shouted.

The vehicles advanced in a staggered line, covering each other. Jack's heart pounded so hard he thought it might burst. He could hear his own breath inside his helmet, ragged and fast.

As the chaos raged on, Jack saw an Iraqi T-72 tank cresting the edge of a sand-covered bunker no more than 300 meters ahead, its turret swinging as if searching for a target. As soon as he heard on the radio, "T-72, one o'clock," an M1 engaged. The blast was instantaneous, deafening. A single sabot round tore through the air and struck the tank dead center. The explosion was violent and immediate, an eruption of fire, smoke, and twisted metal that lit up the desert before his eyes like a flare. The turret rocketed skyward, spinning like a tossed coin, and the hull was engulfed in flames. Jack felt the shockwave, the heat clawing at his face even from that distance. It was over in seconds, but the image was seared into his memory: raw, brutal, and utterly final. A reminder of how fast everything could change.

A few mortars arced through the air and landed less than 100 yards in front of them. The explosions lit up the area in a flash of orange and smoke.

Then, silence.

Cautiously, they approached the bunker Jack had engaged and dug into the now smoldering landscape. Jack kept the .50 cal pointed directly at the structure, fingers ready to pull the trigger again. The bunker was half-collapsed, smoke curling from its entrance.

On one side were two Iraqi soldiers.

One was slumped against the wall, his chest torn open. The other lay face-down, his rifle still clutched in his hands. Blood soaked the sand beneath them.

Jack's breathing paused. His gaze fixed on the scene before him. He was unable to speak. The world narrowed to a darkening tunnel, and all he could see were their faces. One of them couldn't have been older than he was.

He had killed them.

He had pulled the trigger. He had ended their lives.

"Clear!" someone shouted over the radio.

Jack barely heard it. He watched, staring, until Donel came on the radio.

"Mercer. You good?"

"Roger."

Good? Not even close.

The rest of the day blurred. They cleared another bunker. They covered troops taking prisoners, watched as Blackhawks came and went. The desert sun rose high and hot, glaring through the thick smoke. Jack moved like a machine, his body obeying commands while his mind stayed behind in that bunker.

That night, they rallied up with other platoon members near a burned-out convoy. Jack sat alone behind the vehicle, staring out at the desert. The occasional star broke through the smoke that filled the night, and the air had a chill to it.

He accepted a cigarette from his team leader, his hands still shaking. He didn't even smoke. But it gave him something to do, something tangible to hold.

Donel sat down beside him, silent for a while.

"You did what you had to do," he said eventually.

Jack didn't answer.

"You think too much. That'll get you killed."

Jack looked at him. "They were kids, just like me."

Donel looked at Jack, trying to find the right words. "One of the sad facts about war, is that it doesn't care how old you are," he said. "It has zero concern for who it harms or what's destroyed."

Jack didn't reply. He sat there thinking and replaying the scene over and over again in his head.

The next morning, Jack woke with sand in his mouth and a scream caught in his throat. He didn't remember falling asleep. He didn't remember dreaming. But the faces were there.

He didn't tell anyone.

Not then. Not ever.

But Desert Storm was only the beginning.

Jack stayed in. He reenlisted, got promoted, was transferred. The years passed, and the wars changed names, but the rhythm stayed the same: deployment, return, redeployment. Two more tours in Iraq and one to Afghanistan. Each new conflict brought new terrain, new uniforms, new faces. But the fear, the adrenaline, the loss, it all felt the same.

One day, after long patrols searching bunkers and clearing buildings in random little towns, Jack and his unit took up a position outside of Baqubah, about 40 miles north of Baghdad. It was a well-deserved break, or as close as they were going to get. Most of the people, like Jack, were on their third and fourth deployments. Iraq had become familiar to them.

While Jack was cleaning up, doing some laundry, and attempting to eat in peace, a Bedouin came up to their camp with his herd of sheep all around him. Jack saw him coming and quickly put on his flak jacket and helmet and secured his rifle. Other soldiers came over and Jack told them to stand back; he'd go and find out what the man needed.

As Jack walked towards the Bedouin, the man spoke up. "I come in peace," he yelled in a heavy accent. "Taking my sheep to town, to sell."

As Jack got closer, he could see that no one else was with the man, or at least in sight. Jack replied, "If you need to go to Baqubah it's about four miles to the east."

"Yes. Yes. I know. I've been there many, many times. I am Qasim."

He spoke with a kind of happiness. Something rarely heard these days around here.

"How can I assist you then, sir?" Jack asked. He continued to scan the area. He knew that letting his guard down, in these times, could prove costly. Lethal.

"Would you take a sheep?" Qasim's words caught Jack off guard.

"No sir, we don't take sheep."

"Please, I have a sheep for you and your fellow soldiers. A gift."

Jack was only about 10 feet from the man. In his mind he ran through multiple scenarios. Taking a sheep as a gift wasn't one of them.

"Sir ..."

"Please, I am Qasim." He smiled at Jack and slowly raised his arms and pointed all around the area. "I have lived and walked this land all my life. I live in peace. I see you also want to live in peace."

Jack's unit was now on alert, people taking up positions. A couple soldiers had walked about halfway between the camp and Jack. Two vehicles made circles around the area. Jack could hear on the radio it looked all clear. Jack didn't take his eyes off Qasim. He raised his hand up and signaled he was OK back to his team members.

"Qasim, thank you for your offer. But we do not have the resources to care for a sheep."

Qasim smiled and slightly laughed. "No, sir. You and your people can eat him. Roast him over a fire."

He added, "Pick any one you want, sir. They are all healthy and make for a good meal."

Jack radioed back to camp and said, "He wants to give us a sheep to eat."

There was a moment of silence. Then over the radio Jack heard them laugh. "Are you serious? A sheep for us to eat."

"Roger that." Jack replied, "He said I can pick any of them. To roast over a fire."

"That's a negative from higher," the radio came back.

"I want to thank you for your generous offer, Qasim," Jack said. "But we cannot accept one of your beautiful sheep at this time. It is very kind of you to offer."

Qasim continued to smile and slowly walked toward Jack.

"It is OK, sir." He extended his hand to shake. Jack accepted and shook his hand. Qasim had tough hands. Aged by time and hard work. Jack felt more than that, though. Strangely he felt at ease with him. He felt the man meant no ill will or harm.

"You have angels with you, sir," the Bedouin said.

Jack looked at him and thought he was maybe mixing up his English words. So, Jack replied back, "You be safe too, Qasim."

Qasim laughed again, "I will. You are protected, sir. I see angels around you. Light that is good." With that, he turned and called out to his sheep, and they all began to walk with him.

Jack watched as Qasim and his herd of sheep departed back into the desert. He thought of what Qasim had said. Was the man being polite? Was this some kind of old Iraqi goodbye? He pondered this the rest of the night. He didn't share it with any of his fellow soldiers. Just kept it to himself and wondered.

Jack stopped keeping track of the years. The missions bled into each other like ink on wet paper. One day he was patrolling a village in Kandahar, the next he was clearing a compound in Fallujah. Different languages, different enemies, different rules of engagement, but the same smell of cordite, the same ringing in his ears after a blast, the same weight in his chest when they zipped up a body bag.

Occasionally, he would think of Qasim. Did Jack really have angels around him? He had been lucky. Much luckier than some. The injuries Jack sustained were never life-threatening. Angels, though … *Well, it would be nice*, he thought. But Jack believed in being prepared. He ensured his soldiers were prepared and trained. Even doing all of that doesn't stop death. It comes when it wants. Takes who it wants.

He remembered the names of the men lost. Others blurred into initials and call signs. He remembered the sound of a young private sobbing after his first firefight. He remembered the silence of a sergeant who never spoke again after watching his best friend die. He remembered writing letters to families, trying to find words that didn't exist.

Eventually, Jack stopped trying to make sense of it. There was zero sense to be made of it. The war wasn't a series of events anymore. It was a single, endless nightmare. A dream loop where he couldn't awaken.

In 2010, Jack had had enough. 22 years. He did the math and confirmed with headquarters that he had enough years to retire. It was crazy to think about. No more uniform. No more deployments or mentally draining assignments. He could be Jack. But who was Jack, when part of him was stranded in a war-torn world?

8
TIME TO SPEAK

Jack woke to the sounds of birds chattering to one another. Sitting on the edge of his bed, he looked around, as if confirming he was really in his house. The morning light filtered through the blinds in thin, golden stripes, casting shadows across the worn carpet. Dust specks floated in the air, catching the light like tiny ghosts.

Elena was already gone. Her side of the bed was cold, the sheets pulled tight. The house was still. Once again the kind of silence that felt too loud.

He had dreamed of them again.

The two men in the bunker. The way their bodies had folded in on themselves, like broken marionettes. The way the blood had soaked into the sand, dark and fast, like the earth itself was trying to swallow the memory. He could still smell it all, burnt metal, sweat, something sharp and coppery. He could still hear the silence that followed the gunfire. Not peace. Not relief. Just absence. A void.

He rubbed his hands over his face, then stood slowly, his joints stiff and aching, as if he'd aged a decade overnight. The floor was cold beneath his feet as he walked to the bathroom, each step deliberate, like he was trying not to wake something inside him.

He turned on the tap and splashed cold water on his face. It shocked him but not enough. Nothing ever did.

He looked up at the mirror.

Grey threaded his beard now. Lines had carved themselves deep around his eyes, like the years had carved their story into his skin. But the eyes themselves, that was what stopped him. Same color. Same shape. Same haunted stare.

He didn't recognize the man, but he knew the look.

He had told Elena bits and pieces. Enough to explain the nightmares, the mood swings, the way he sometimes drifted off mid-conversation like he was somewhere else entirely. He'd said he'd seen combat. That he'd lost people. That it had changed him.

But he'd never gone in-depth. It was etched in his mind; he could recite the events second by second. He didn't know if he was protecting her or protecting himself. Maybe both.

He gripped the edge of the sink, knuckles white, and took a deep breath. The kind that was supposed to steady you. It didn't.

Some mornings were like this. Some mornings, the war hit you before the coffee did.

When it was Jack's turn to speak at the Veteran's Group, he hesitated. The others had shared their truths. Ray's panic attacks, Denise's guilt, Carlos's daughter holding his hand in the mall. Malik's numbness. Frank's ghosts from Vietnam.

Jack's mouth felt dry. His thoughts tangled. What could he say that wouldn't sound small compared to their problems? He felt the familiar pressure in his chest, the urge to deflect, to say something vague and move on. *You don't belong here*, the voice in his head whispered. *Your pain isn't enough. You're just tired. Just stressed. Not broken.*

But—just like he'd practiced—he caught it. That voice wasn't truth. It was fear dressed up as logic.

He looked down at his hands and around the circle. Then he spoke.

"I've been in multiple firefights," he said, clearing a grumbling sound from his throat. "Death became a constant presence. After a while, I accepted it as a part of war. The only question was whether it was your time or not."

Jack took a deep breath and slowly let it out. His hands began to shake, and his foot was tapping like a jackrabbit's.

"But it's the first two men I killed in Desert Storm that haunt me," he went on. "My first, during too many deployments and too many firefights. I was 21.”

The room went still.

“I remember everything. The way the air smelled. The way the muzzle flashes lit up the desert. The way the bodies looked when we reached the bunker.”

He paused, his voice tight.

“I didn't feel proud. I didn't feel brave. I felt ... empty. Like something had been taken from me.”

He looked down at his hands.

“I never told anyone. Not really. I buried it. But it's still there. Every night. Every time I close my eyes.”

He looked up.

“I think that was the moment I stopped being a kid. And I've been trying to figure out who I am ever since.”

After the meeting, no one said much. They didn't have to. Ray gave him a nod. Denise touched his shoulder. Malik looked at him like he was seeing him for the first time.

Jack walked out into the sunlight, the air crisp and clean. For the first time in decades, he was truly vulnerable. He had released some of his demons. He thought of his mom and how she had battled her own demons. How she overcame them and was able to enjoy the final years of her life with family.

He hoped he could be that strong.

9
CARLA

Carla Margarette Stallings was born on a rainy morning in June, 1944, in Seattle, Washington, while the world was still at war. Her father, Doyle Stallings, had enlisted in the Army and was serving in the Pacific. Her mother, Louise, worked part-time as a seamstress and full-time at being angry. They were young, poor, and unraveling by the time Carla was old enough to walk.

When Carla was almost eight, Doyle packed a suitcase and made the tough decision to leave. His marriage to Louise wasn't working out, and that was putting it nicely. He said he was going back home to Texas, where his family roots were. Louise didn't stop him. She just stood in the doorway with Carla and, in one arm, partially resting on her thin hip, their baby boy Kenny. Louise didn't watch for long; she had other things to attend to. But Carla stood there for a while, holding in tears so she wouldn't make her mom mad. She watched her father disappear into the grey Seattle mist and the dust of their gravel road.

It would be years before Carla was able to see her dad again.

Louise moved the family south to Sacramento, California, chasing a promise of work, and to be near her sister. They ended up in a three-bedroom house on O Street, a few blocks away from the church they'd all attend and the school Carla and Kenny would attend. Louise took a job with the government and did seamstress work on the side. But the change of scenery and new job did nothing to limit or ease her anger.

Carla's baby brother, Kenny, was a handful, and she felt that watching him was a full-time job. By then, Carla had already learned to stay quiet, to move carefully, to read her mother's moods like weather patterns, and she did her best to teach Kenny to do so, too.

When she was younger, she had contracted polio, which led to scoliosis. She spent weeks in the hospital, her tiny body wrapped in braces, her muscles refusing to obey. The nurses were kind at the hospital; it was refreshing. The doctors were distant. Her mother only visited twice.

When Carla came home, she was different. She was in an upper body brace for months, confined to her bed. She was slower. Fragile. And Louise didn't like fragile things.

"You're not going to be a cripple," she snapped one day, yanking Carla's arm when she stumbled. "You're going to walk like a normal girl, or you're not going to walk at all."

The abuse wasn't always physical. Sometimes it was silent. Sometimes it was shameful. Louise would complain if she limped, yell at her, "Don't be gimpy!" and tell her no man would ever want her. She'd scream about Doyle, about how he'd left her with "two mouths and no money," and how Carla was just like him—weak, selfish, ungrateful.

Carla learned to disappear inside herself. She read books. She got stronger. Her spine fused with bone straightened. She dreamed of escaping.

By the time she was 16, Carla had a plan. She would graduate, enlist in the Navy, and never look back. She wanted to wear the uniform. She wanted to serve as a nurse. She wanted to be someone.

She told her mother one night over dinner.

Louise laughed. A sharp, bitter sound. "You? In the Navy? With that back? They don't take broken girls."

Carla didn't argue. She just nodded and finished her meal. But something inside her cracked that night. Not broke, just cracked. Enough to let the light in.

She met James Mercer at school when she was 17. He was tall, soft-spoken, with dark hair and a quiet sadness in his eyes. He'd moved to Sacramento from back east with his parents, who were devout Catholics and strict as stone, similar to Louise.

James was different. He didn't flinch at her health concerns. He didn't ask about her past. He just listened. He made her laugh. He made her feel seen.

They started dating in secret. Both families would've disapproved; the two of them were too fast, too serious, and there was too much sin in the air. But Carla didn't care. For the first time in her life, she felt like she was writing her own story.

Then she got pregnant.

The wedding was small and tense. Carla wore a borrowed dress. James looked like he was trying not to run. Their parents refused to attend the ceremony.

Carla was 19. James was 20.

They moved to San Jose, where James found some work, and he continued his efforts to be an artist. Carla stayed home with the baby girl they named Elizabeth. A year later, Michael was born.

For a while, they tried. They really did.

James worked long hours. Carla cooked, cleaned, and tried to be the kind of wife the church said she should be. But the cracks in their marriage grew wider with each passing year. James spent more time away from home. Carla cried more. Arguments became the norm. The dream was crashing down all around Carla.

When she found out she was pregnant again, she told James over dinner. He didn't say much. They ate in silence as their two little ones played.

She was six months pregnant when James said he wanted a divorce and was leaving. That same day he was packed up and was gone. She was alone. Two toddlers, and a baby on the way. No job. No degree. No family nearby. Just a small apartment full of silence, and a heart full of fear.

In March of 1970, she gave birth to a little boy, Jack. Her brother was there to help her; he had just gotten out of the Army. Together they packed up the kids and moved back to Sacramento. Louise was still there, older but no softer. Carla was able to get a job as a secretary with a local credit union and get into a little house on P street.

Carla made attempts to visit her mother and have the kids be a part of her life, but Louise was cold even towards them and her criticism continued. "You're just like him," Louise said one night, cold and bitter. "You think you're special, but you're not. You're just another girl who got knocked up and left behind."

Carla didn't respond. She just held her children tighter. They left and walked back to her little house on P Street, Elizabeth and Michael stomping on leaves along the sidewalk. Jack in her arms.

Sometimes, after her shift, she'd sit on the porch with a cigarette and stare at the sky. She'd think about the Navy. About the ocean. About the life she almost had.

And she'd cry.

Quietly. So, the kids wouldn't hear.

The memories of the house on P Street were vague for Jack. The years that followed were a blur of back-and-forth trips along I-40 between California and Texas.

He didn't understand then or even through most of his younger years what his mom had gone through and what she had to deal with. Her demons were a mystery to him.

But he knew now.

He remembered the way she disappeared for days sometimes. The way she'd come back hollow-eyed and jittery. He didn't know the word "addiction" back then. He just knew she would return different. Sadder. More stressed.

He remembered the time he waited at the door to their house in Wellington. Waiting for her to come home. He didn't have a key yet. A family friend eventually came by and said, "Your mom had to go away for a few days, so you'll be staying with us." He always assumed it was work-related.

It wasn't until his sophomore year in high school that his stepdad, Gary, took him to visit Carla in a recovery center. She looked thinner than he remembered, her eyes clearer but rimmed with something fragile. In the quiet of the visitation room, she began to explain—not just the addiction, but the ache beneath it. She spoke of the nights she couldn't sleep, the weight of shame, the way the pills had started as relief and ended as a cage. Her voice trembled at times, but she didn't look away.

Jack listened, still and silent, his hands in his lap. He didn't interrupt and didn't ask any questions. In that hour, all the puzzle pieces came together—the missed birthdays, the sudden disappearances, the way she used to smile like she was trying to convince herself she was okay. It all made sense now, and though it didn't erase the past, it softened something in him. For the first time, he saw her not as the woman who left unexpectedly and hid secrets, but as someone who had been lost.

After the visit, Jack carried a quiet heaviness with him. The kind that settled in his chest and never quite left. Seeing his mom like that—honest, vulnerable, trying—had cracked something open. He wanted to believe it was a turning point. For a while, it was. She was more present and often cheerful. She sounded clearer. She even laughed again. But addiction wasn't linear, and neither was recovery.

Carla kept battling her demons, sometimes winning, often not. There were relapses—some small, some terrifying. Jack, by then in the Army, would drop everything when things got bad. He took emergency leave more than once, flying home with a quickly packed overnight bag and a knot in his stomach, hoping this time would be different. He'd sit with his sister in ER waiting rooms, argue with insurance reps, beg intake coordinators at rehab centers to find her a bed. He tried everything—detox programs, outpatient therapy, even holistic retreats. But nothing seemed to stick back then.

Each time she slipped, it felt like watching someone drown in slow motion. And Jack, trained to handle chaos on the battlefield, felt utterly powerless. He never stopped trying, but a part of him began to brace for the worst. Not out of apathy, but out of exhaustion. Loving someone through addiction was like holding your breath underwater—eventually, something had to give.

Years later, in February of 2011, Jack got the call late one night from his uncle. His mom had had a massive stroke and was in the hospital in Big Spring.

The next morning, Jack, Elena, and the girls loaded up the car and headed for Big Spring. It was a four-hour drive. Jack couldn't help but think, *Is this it, is Mom going to die?* She had overcome so much in her life, Jack felt she had to pull through. This was just another bump in the road for her, he hoped. He silently prayed for it.

Carla's hospital room was cold, filled with the low hum of machines and the quiet murmur of medical staff discussing vitals and protocols. Jack stood at the foot of the bed, tuning them all out. His mother lay still, her body thin and pale, tubes and wires snaking from her arms and mouth. Her chest rose and fell with the rhythm of the ventilator, but the doctors had already told him she was gone. Her brain had stopped responding. Her body just hadn't caught on yet.

Uncle Kenny stood beside him, silent, a steady presence. Jack stared at his mother, willing her to wake up, to open her eyes, to make the decision for him. But it was his to make. It had always been his.

Then, through the noise, he heard it, a soft, faint voice, like a whisper carried in the wind.

"Please let me go."

He looked around. It was murmured right in his ear. But no one was standing by him. No one else had heard it. They were still talking about charts and timelines. He looked back at her, and something in him broke.

"Okay," he said quietly, and a tear began to run down his cheek.

He signed the forms. Half a dozen signatures that felt like a betrayal and a mercy all at once. Then he left the hospital with Uncle Kenny, the weight of the moment pressing down on his chest.

An hour later, the doctor called. Carla had passed away, officially. But Jack already knew. She had been gone even before she asked him to let her go.

Years later, in the Veteran's support group, when it was his turn to speak, Jack shared a bit about Carla.

"My mom was a fighter. Not the kind with fists. The kind who kept going when everything told her to stop. She was abused. She was abandoned. She was broken in ways I didn't understand until I got older."

He paused.

"She wanted to join the Navy. Her mom said no. She got pregnant young. Married a man who left her. Raised three kids on her own. And still, somehow, she loved us. She found a way to become a nurse, and in her later years she was able to enjoy life with her granddaughters."

He looked around the circle. "I used to be angry at her. For the drugs. For the disappearances. For the way she'd vanish when we needed her most. But now ... I think she was just trying to survive. Like all of us."

After the meeting, Jack sat in his truck for a long time, staring at the steering wheel. He thought about calling his sister. He hadn't spoken to her in months. She had her own scars. Her own version of their mother. Jack leaned his head back on the seat, the afternoon light slanting through the window, casting long shadows across the parking lot. The hum of traffic on highway 101 was rhythmic—almost hypnotic. Something about the stillness of the moment pulled him backward, into a memory he hadn't visited in years:

Wichita Falls, Texas. He must've been eight, maybe nine. One night stood out more than the rest from his and his mom's short, difficult stay there. The house they lived in had no air conditioning—just open windows with warped screens that barely kept the bugs out. The air was thick and unmoving, the kind of heat that clung to your skin and made sleep feel like a chore.

His mom had just come home after a long day chasing leads that led nowhere. She was trying to sell something—Jack couldn't remember what exactly—but whatever it was, it wasn't selling. She walked in with that tired smile she wore when she didn't want him to worry. But Jack saw it. The pain behind her eyes. The weight she carried.

They sat together on the black vinyl couch in their small living room. Jack remembered the feel of it—sticky against his legs, the way it squeaked when you shifted your weight. The walls were covered in faux wood paneling, seams visible where the sheets didn't quite meet. Some of it was peeling away from the wall. He'd thought about fixing it once, if only he had a hammer and a finishing nail.

His mom asked him to go next door and use the neighbor's phone to call his uncle—she wanted to know if his brother was over there. Jack didn't ask why. He just nodded, got up, and stepped out into the warm night air. The red brick path was uneven, like everything else in their lives at the time. He walked past the sagging sidewalk and up the neighbor's driveway, nerves fluttering in his chest. He'd never met the woman who lived there.

His first knock was weak. He hoped no one would answer. But then he knocked again, a little louder. The porch light flicked on, casting a deep orange glow over the small stoop. The screen door creaked open and a soft, older voice asked, "May I help you?"

Mrs. Smith. That was her name. She looked like someone's grandmother—kind eyes, silver hair, a floral blouse. Jack explained that he lived next door and needed to use the phone. She didn't hesitate. "Well, the phone's over on that table," she said, pointing to a dark wood shelf across from the TV.

Her living room was small, like theirs, but neater. The furniture was old but well-kept, and the walls were covered in framed pictures of dogs. Two photos of men in military uniforms hung above the television— sharp-looking, proud. Jack dialed the number, let it ring eight times, then hung up. "No one home, I guess," Mrs. Smith said kindly. Jack thanked her and made his way back home.

His mom was still on the couch, talking to herself. Jack started doing that, too, years later. Sometimes, his own voice was the only one that made sense. "No answer," he told her. She handed him a card with another number. "Try this one," she said.

So back he went. Same path, same orange light, same nervous knock. This time, he noticed a gnome in the yard—red hat, white beard, missing an arm. Somehow, that made it creepy. Mrs. Smith opened the door before he could knock again. "Need the phone again?" she asked with a smile.

"Yes, ma'am."

He dialed the second number. This time, his aunt answered. Chris was there. Mission accomplished. He thanked Mrs. Smith again, and as he turned to leave, she asked, "What does your family do?"

"My mom's a saleswoman. I'm just in school," he replied, as if a fifth grader could be anything else.

Then she asked something unexpected. "Would you and your mom like some ice cream? I also have some extra canned goods you could have." Jack nodded in acceptance and thanked her.

Jack returned home with a paper bag nearly as big as his chest. His mom looked up, surprised. "Mrs. Smith gave us some food and ice cream," he said. "And Chris is at Uncle Kenny's."

She stared at the bag for a moment, then told him to put it away and have a bite to eat. A few minutes later, Jack saw her slip out the front door and walk toward Mrs. Smith's house.

He must've dozed off on the couch. When he woke, his mom was back. Her eyes were red. "Did you visit with Mrs. Smith?" he asked.

"Yes, I did," she said softly. "She's a wonderful woman."

Jack told her there was a bowl of green beans in the fridge for her. She smiled. "Thank you."

Later, she brought out two bowls of peach ice cream, and they sat together, eating in silence. It was one of those rare, gentle moments— sweet, fleeting, and safe.

Then she told him they were moving again. Back to Wellington. She had a lead on a nursing job. Jack just nodded. He was used to it by then.

"You should get some sleep," she said. "We've got a busy day tomorrow."

Jack, now decades older, blinked and came back to the present. That night had stayed with him—not because of the hardship, but because of the kindness. The quiet resilience of his mother. The generosity of a neighbor. The way a bowl of ice cream could feel like a lifeline.

Some memories never fade. They just wait for the right moment to return.

One of Jack's final memories of his mom was when he, Elena, and the girls stopped by the nursing home she was in, before heading out of town and back home. As they stepped into her room, Carla was asleep on her bed. Jack gently rubbed her leg.

Carla woke, and a smile as beautiful and as big as ever appeared on her face once she realized her granddaughters and kids were there. It was a moment of pure love. Jack knew this was what his mom needed. Through everything she had been through, Jack's mom was just as beautiful as she was as a teenager. Her skin as soft as silk and eyes crystal blue.

That night was the last time he would see her alive and returning smiles.

He wished he could drive to the cemetery in Wellington, Texas.

He hadn't cried at the funeral. He made a humorous comment about his mom popping out of the coffin—after all, she was a fighter and had beaten death a few times.

But now, sitting in a parking lot, he felt the tears come. Not just for her, but for the girl she used to be. The girl who wanted to be more. He hoped she had found what she needed.

10
THE SEARCH FOR WORK

Jack had always believed in hard work. It was one of the few things that made sense to him: show up, do your job, earn your keep. It was how he survived in the Army, how he made it through grad school, how he landed a high school teaching job and then a government job after retiring from active duty.

But belief didn't pay the bills.

He had resigned from his federal job. After his time in the mental health unit and the outpatient program, he knew it was the right decision. The environment was toxic, pervaded with micromanagement, backbiting, and a culture of fear disguised as "accountability". He'd tried to stick it out. Told himself he could help change the culture and that he could endure anything. But the stress had started to feel like combat again—a tight chest, sleepless nights, the constant sense that something was about to explode.

So he walked away.

At first, he felt like he had failed. Earlier he had left a teaching position in which he had been very successful. He was awarded teacher of the year once and had been a runner-up another. But after resigning his federal job, he had no salary and was living in one of the priciest places in the country.

Jack told himself he was now free of the stress and nonsense. He was indeed relieved. He slept a little better. Ate better. Spent more time with Elena.

Eventually he managed to get a good position he enjoyed at a beautiful and luxurious hotel in Sonoma. But his job as Assistant Director of Human Resources was short-lived after the pandemic hit. The resort closed temporarily in the spring, furloughing most of the staff with the hope that things would bounce back by summer. But summer came and went, and guests didn't return. Furloughs turned into layoffs. Jack got the call on a Friday morning: polite, apologetic, final. There was no severance, just a thank you and a promise to keep his résumé on file.

Jack tried to stay optimistic. He updated his professional profiles, polished his résumé, and started applying for jobs. But the hospitality industry had been gutted. HR roles were scarce, and the competition was fierce.

Weeks turned into months. Interviews came and went, most ending with a polite rejection or no response at all. He picked up part-time gigs doing odd jobs, but nothing steady. Nothing like a career.

Now, more than a year later, Jack was still searching. The weight of it pressed on him daily—not just the financial strain, but the sense of lost identity. He had always taken pride in work, in helping people navigate their careers, in building teams and solving problems. He tried to stay busy, tried to stay hopeful, but it was hard.

Savings started to shrink. Retirement pay helped, but it wasn't enough. Not with a mortgage, insurance, and groceries that seemed to cost more every week. Work was a must.

Jack had a master's degree in business administration. He had 22 years of military leadership experience. He had managed teams, budgets, and crises. He had letters of recommendation, an impressive résumé, and a professional profile that looked like it belonged to someone who had it all figured out.

Borderline desperate, he started applying to all kinds of jobs, ones out of his specialty. The positions he applied to included program manager roles, analyst positions, nonprofit leadership jobs, even recruiting positions. He tailored his cover letters. He researched every organization. He practiced interview questions in the mirror.

And he got interviews. Lots of them.

The first one was with a large wine distributor near Napa. The organization seemed solid, had great reviews and nice employee support packages. Jack felt good about it. The first interview went well. The second was with the executive director and a couple board members, who seemed to smile too much and asked him how he "handled stress, handled difficult situations, and how he dealt with adversity."

Jack wanted to laugh. Or scream.

"I've had a lot of practice with all three," he started. "Between my time in the military, deployments, and the transitions that came after retirement, I've learned that stress and adversity are part of life—you can't avoid them, but you can choose how you respond. When I'm under pressure, I focus on staying calm and breaking the situation down into manageable parts. In the Army, we were trained to assess, prioritize, and act—especially in high-stakes environments. That mindset stuck with me. Whether it's a medical emergency in the field or a tight deadline in the civilian world, I stay grounded by focusing on what I can control."

He went on. "I also believe in preparation. The more prepared I am, the more confident I feel, and that reduces stress. But I've also learned to adapt when things don't go as planned. Life has thrown me curveballs—injuries, career changes, personal loss—and I've had to pivot more than once. What's helped me most is staying resilient, leaning on my support system, and keeping a sense of purpose."

He took a breath. "At the end of the day, I don't see adversity as something to fear," he said. "It's something to learn from. Every challenge I've faced has made me stronger, more empathetic, and more capable. I am confident I can handle the challenges that may come with this role."

They nodded politely. Took notes. Promised to follow up.

They didn't.

With a worldwide alcohol distributor, he had five different interviews. Each time with a different group of managers. New questions, but the same ending: "We'll be in touch."

They actually did contact Jack again, to request yet another interview. This time he had enough. No more interviews. He called the hiring manager and discussed it; his patience had worn out.

"If you can't decide if I'm the right person after five interviews, then apparently I'm not. Sorry, but no more interviews," he told her.

She replied with the usual professional corporate answer he had come accustomed to hearing.

The following day, he received the very familiar email kindly thanking him for his time and informing him they were moving forward with another candidate.

He shook his head in silence and then quietly laughed.

Next was a state agency. It was for a position as a veteran outreach coordinator, a job that looked like it had been written for him. He made it to the final round. Three interviews. A panel. A writing sample. A background check.

Then silence.

He followed up. Once. Twice. A third time.

Finally, a form email: "We've decided to move forward with another candidate." No explanation. No feedback. Just another door slammed shut.

By this point, Jack was angry. Not just disappointed, but furious and annoyed. After yet another interview, he sat in his truck, gripping the steering wheel so hard his knuckles turned white. He'd just spent an hour explaining how he'd managed logistics for a battalion in Afghanistan, how he'd coordinated emergency evacuations, how he'd led teams in difficult situations, and the hiring manager had asked him if he was "comfortable with spreadsheets."

Spreadsheets.

He wanted to ask them if they had any idea what it was like to have such in-depth experience, be twice as qualified as required, and then be told you were overqualified, underqualified, or just "not the right fit". He wanted to ask why they had invited him to interview three times if they were just going to ghost him. He wanted to ask if they could see the desperation behind his calm answers. If they could hear the clock ticking in his head every time they said, "We'll be in touch."

At home, he tried to hide it. But Elena saw through him.

"You're angry," she said one night, sitting beside him on the couch.

"I'm tired," he replied.

"Of what?"

"Of pretending I'm the guy these companies need. Of jumping through hoops. Of being told I'm not exactly what they're looking for, or hear you're highly qualified, but … Trying to prove I belong in a world that doesn't know what to do with people like me."

She didn't say anything. Just took his hand and held it.

Claire, their rescue dog, trotted quietly into the room and placed her two front paws on Jack's knee. Her eyes were soft, steady, and knowing. Jack reached down and scratched behind her ears, feeling the warmth of her fur and the quiet comfort she always seemed to offer without asking for anything in return. She didn't need explanations. She just stayed close, like she knew when he needed comforting, his silent furry companion through the noise. Peace for a moment.

The next morning, he started to question everything. He counted up all of the jobs he had applied to, confirmations of applications received, requests for interviews, number of interviews, and how many times he'd been ghosted, left clueless.

There were over 100 jobs. There had been 26 initial interviews with different organizations. With 19 of them he had gone on to a second, third, fourth, and, once, even a fifth interview. He had applied to positions all over California and in a few other states.

He began to doubt himself. Maybe he wasn't as capable as he thought. Maybe the world had moved on and left him behind. Maybe the skills that had once made him valuable were now just relics of a different time.

He felt like clicking the "submit" button was a futile gesture of desperation and hope. *What I am doing?* he thought over and over again. Was it worth it? Was he ready to go back to work? Could he sit in an office again, surrounded by people who'd never seen the things he'd seen? Could he take orders from someone who'd never led anyone through anything more dangerous than a budget meeting?

But he had to. He and Elena couldn't live on pride.

Jack took a deep breath, closed his eyes, and the world fell away.

The wind rushed past him like a river of freedom, tugging at his hair and clothes, carrying the scent of wild sage and sun-warmed earth. His heartbeat matched the thunder of hooves beside him—raw, rhythmic, and alive. A mustang, a streak of muscle and fire, galloped just inches away, its mane whipping like a banner in the wind. Jack didn't need to see it. He could feel it. Every stride of the horse echoed in his chest, every snort and breath a call to something ancient and untamed within him.

Jack's feet pounded the ground in sync with the horse's, with the reckless abandon of someone who had let go. Dust rose around them in golden clouds, catching the morning light like sparks. The earth was uneven, but Jack trusted it. Trusted the rhythm. Trusted the mustang.

For a moment, there was no separation between boy and beast. They were one force, one spirit, racing across the open plain. Jack's arms moved in rhythm with the gallop, his breath deep and wild. He didn't think. He didn't plan. He just ran—eyes closed, heart open, soul flying.

And in that moment, he was free. Free of wanting, of needing, and of desperation.

"Do you ever think we were trained for a world that doesn't exist anymore?" Jack asked his best friend and old Army buddy, Graham, who was in town doing some work for a private security firm. They sat at a small café in Petaluma, sipping bitter coffee and swapping stories.

"All the time. But that doesn't mean we're useless. It just means we have to find new ways to matter."

Jack looked out his window. "I'm trying. I really am."

"I know you are. Just don't let this system make you forget who you are."

That night, Jack sat down with Elena and opened up a spreadsheet—yes, he was comfortable with spreadsheets—but this time it was not for a job but to track his applications, interviews, and rejections in a tangible way. He took all his notes and put the company, the position, if they had reached out, when he reached out, and the interviews. He wanted to see it all laid out, nice and neat, to make sense of the chaos. It was sobering. But it also gave him a strange sense of control.

He added a column entitled, "Lessons Learned". He began to analyze the experience:

Don't chase roles that don't align with your values.

Ask better questions in interviews.

Trust your gut when something feels off.

You are not your job title.

It wasn't much. But it was something. And for now, something was enough.

As he closed his laptop, he reminisced about how life had been in his and Graham's younger days. Simpler, definitely. And a bit wilder.

11
THE HORSEMEN

Germany, 1990

Germany in the early '90s was a strange and beautiful place for a young American soldier. The Cold War had just ended, the wall had come down, and the world felt like it was shifting beneath everyone's boots. Jack was stationed at a small base near Mainz, and after arrival it hadn't taken him long to find his people–Sam, Stone, and Graham. Together with Jack, they were known around the post and beyond as *The Horsemen*. Not because they were apocalyptic troublemakers, though trouble did occasionally find them, but because wherever they went, they rode together. Tight. Loyal. Unshakable.

They trained hard, becoming experts at their jobs, working hard to prove themselves, and lived for the weekends. Each gained the respect of senior leaders. With that came a degree of leeway. While others got crap details, the four of them were given better assignments.

When the work week was over, they'd hop trains to Frankfurt, Wiesbaden, or smaller villages tucked along the Rhine, enjoying good beer, great music, and making the kind of memories that only come from being young, wild, and far from home. They had each other's backs in the field and in the streets, and that bond was forged in fire, sweat, and the occasional minor altercation at a bar.

But nothing compared to the night in Rüdesheim.

Rüdesheim was a sleepy little wine village by day, nestled along the river, with cobblestone streets and timber-framed buildings. But by night, especially on a Friday, it came alive with music, tourists, and locals looking to blow off steam. The *Horsemen* had been there once before. It had been a great time, a quiet getaway from the regular-Joe hangout spots that felt crowded and too loud. But this night was different.

They were at a bar tucked into a narrow street, the kind of place with low ceilings, thick smoke, and a jukebox that hadn't been updated since the '70s. The beer was cold, the shots were flowing, and the four of them were in rare form, laughing, telling stories, and drawing attention without even trying. That's when a few members of a local gang showed up.

They weren't wearing leather jackets or flashing colors—this wasn't that kind of gang. These were locals, all German, and everyone in town knew who they were. They were the kind of guys who grew up together, never left, and made sure everyone knew it. Their look was understated—jeans, boots, tight-fitting shirts—but their presence was loud. They walked in with a swagger that came from years of getting away with things. The kind of confidence that came from knowing the cops wouldn't bother, and most people wouldn't dare.

The gang arrived and acted as if they owned the place. At first, it was just looks. Then words. Then one of them shoulder-checked Sam on the way back from the bar. Sam, a wiry and fiery dude from Florida, didn't flinch. He just stared the guy down, calm and steady. But the tension was thick, and it didn't take long to for the atmosphere to snap.

One of the gang members standing to the side of Sam threw a punch. Sam saw it coming and leaned back as the fist went by. Then another grabbed Sam from behind. In a flurry of jostling and cursing, the gang dragged him out the front door and into the street.

Through the commotion, they could hear Sam yell, "Jack! Graham! Stone!"

Jack, Graham, and Stone didn't hesitate. They bolted outside, the door slamming behind them, and what they saw stopped them cold. The street was filled—20, maybe 25 members of the local gang, circling Sam like wolves. But the *Horsemen* didn't blink. They rushed into the crowd and began leveling the playing field.

It was total chaos.

Jack grabbed the first guy he saw, slammed his head into a steel fence, then spun and drove another into a brick wall with a sickening crunch. Graham was a blur—fast, brutal, and efficient. He smashed a guy's head through a bar window, sending glass and blood flying. Stone moved like a machine, dropping one dude after another with clean, punishing blows. He fought like he was built for it—calm, focused, devastating.

Sam, now free, was a force of nature. He picked one of the gang members up and literally threw him over a wrought-iron fence like a sack of potatoes. Another came at him with a bottle, and Sam caught his wrist mid-swing, twisted, and dropped him with a single punch, then followed it up with a hard kick to the chest.

They were outnumbered five to one, but it didn't matter. The *Horsemen* fought like they were a battalion of 200, each one eliminating one or two gang members at a time. At times, each of them was surrounded, taking on three, four, even five guys at once. They didn't back down. They'd knock out the closest one and then go after another.

The street echoed with shouts, the crunch of fists on bone, the crash of bodies against cars and walls. Locals watched from windows, some cheering, others calling the police. And then, in the distance, they heard it, the wail of sirens.

"Polizei!" someone shouted.

The gang scattered, those that could run, some limping and most bleeding. The *Horsemen* didn't wait around either. They ran, ducking into alleys, diving behind bushes, crawling under parked cars. Jack's knuckles were bleeding and his ribs ached from a couple blows he had taken, but he was grinning and laughing. Sam began to laugh, too.

Graham tried to be serious. "You guys need to shut up," he said, but a smile was on his face as well.

"Damn it! I didn't finish my beer," quipped Stone, and they all laughed, then caught themselves and went quiet.

They moved like ghosts through the village, sticking to the shadows, hearts pounding. Eventually, they made it to the train station, breathless. The platform was empty and calm, but the night was still humming with adrenaline. A train pulled in, and without a word they climbed aboard, collapsing into the seats like survivors of a war.

They ducked down below the window until the train had left

Rüdesheim, only sitting up once they were safely out of town. For a long moment, no one spoke. Then Sam let out a big whoop. "Hell, yeah!" he exulted. "No one's going to believe this night."

Jack leaned back, wiping sweat from his brow, and smiled. "Good. Let's keep it that way."

They rode in silence, the train wheels clacking on the tracks beneath them, the lights of the village fading into the distance. They were tired, scraped up a bit, and probably lucky to not be in a German jail cell, but they were together and had a hell of a tale. And that was all that mattered.

As the train rumbled through the dark countryside, the adrenaline began to wear off, replaced by the dull throb of their bruises. Jack looked around at his brothers: Sam rubbing his shoulder, Stone quietly looking at his torn shirt, and Graham leaning back with his eyes closed, blood that wasn't his smeared across one temple.

The silence wasn't awkward. It was peaceful. The kind of silence that only comes after something real, something raw. They had walked into the fire and come out the other side, not unscathed, but even more alive.

Jack reached into his jacket and pulled out a crumpled cigarette pack. He lit one, took a drag, then passed it to Sam without a word. It made its way around the group, each of them taking a moment, a breath, a memory.

"Think word will get back to base?" Stone finally asked, his voice low and dry.

Sam snorted. "Only if they find the bodies."

They all laughed, quiet and tired, but genuinely. The kind of laugh that had a cheer and a "hell, yes" entwined with it. The kind that stitched wounds up better than any medic ever could.

The train slowed as it neared Mainz. The lights of the city shimmered in the distance, soft and golden. Jack felt a strange ache in his chest, not pain, not fear, but something deeper. A knowing. That this night, this fight, this bond, they'd carry it forever. He thought how no one would believe a night like this happened, how they came out on top against ridiculous odds. It was a tall tale for sure and one he'd never forget.

They didn't share with anyone else what happened in Rüdesheim. It became one of those unspoken legends, a story told in glances and inside jokes. A mark they all shared, invisible but undeniable.

Back at the barracks, they cleaned up in silence. Jack stood under the shower, watching the water swirl down the drain, and thought about how close they'd come to disaster. But he didn't regret it. Not for a second.

Later that night, they gathered in the room Jack, Sam, and Graham shared, beers in hand, each one's experience blooming in conversation like the finale of a fireworks display. Someone put on a music CD, and they sat there, listening and laughing.

They weren't just soldiers. They weren't just friends. They were *Horsemen*, and that meant a deep brotherhood. And in that moment, in that quiet room filled with the hum of music and the weight of what they'd just gone through, they knew one thing for sure: no matter where life took them, no matter the wars, the years, the distance, they'd always be able to count on one another when needed.

12
THE JOB OFFER

The email came on a Thursday morning, just after sunrise. Jack was sitting at the kitchen table, sipping lukewarm coffee, scrolling through job boards out of habit more than hope. When the notification popped up, he almost didn't open it. He'd been ghosted so many times that even good news felt like a setup.

But this one read differently.

Subject: Offer of Employment – University of North Texas Health Science Center

He read it twice. Then a third time. It was real. A full-time position in the Office of the President. Good salary. Nice perks. A leadership role. They wanted him.

He stared at the screen for a while, re-reading the offer, heart pounding. He looked at the job description multiple times, reviewed his interview notes. This was real.

He knew he had applied to it. He remembered the interviews. But a part of him had to confirm this was real. Not spam. Not the old recruiting run-around. A real job offer.

He waited for Elena to wake up. As she stepped into the dining room, he turned his laptop towards her. "They offered me the job," he said.

She blinked, groggy. "What job?"

"UNT. Fort Worth."

She slowly sat down beside him. "Texas?"

He nodded.

She didn't say anything for a long time. Then finally she asked about the job and what he would be doing.

"I'd be working in the President's office creating their new department for After-Action Review. That's crazy, right?"

Elena nodded and was happy for him. But Texas?

They talked about it more that night. And the next. And the one after that. They had some friends there. Jack had history there. He had to give the university an answer by Monday.

They loved Marin County. The redwoods. The fog. The trails behind their house. The farmer's market on Saturdays. The ocean, just a short drive away. They had put a lot of work into their little home. They had made it theirs. A sanctuary from the world, and a place filled with memories. It was home.

But it was also brutally expensive. And Jack hadn't had a steady income in over a year. Elena had started working as a delivery driver at night. The stress was starting to show in the lines around her eyes, in the way she sighed when she thought he wasn't listening.

"I hate this," she said one night, sitting on the back deck with a glass of wine. "I hate that we have to leave just to survive." Claire was curled up against her.

"I know," Jack said.

"I'm angry. Not at you. Just ... at everything."

He nodded. "Me, too."

Monday came quickly. It had been a fast weekend with far too many discussions about moving and what-ifs. In the end though, it was an offer. They both agreed he would accept it. That afternoon he called their real estate agent. He told her the news, and they scheduled a time for her to come out and start the paperwork.

A few days later, it was Jack's birthday. He didn't want a party. He didn't want cake. He just wanted to forget the heaviness of the last year. He started drinking around noon, just a beer, then another. By dinner, he'd moved on to whiskey. By the time Elena got home, he was sitting on the back patio, glassy-eyed, a half-empty bottle beside him.

"Really?" she said, stepping outside. "This is how you want to spend your birthday?"

"It's the only thing that makes me feel normal," he muttered.

She crossed her arms. "You've been drinking more, Jack. You don't even see it."

"I'm not drunk," he snapped. "I'm relaxed. There's a difference."

"No, there's not. Not anymore."

He stood up too fast, swaying slightly. "You think I want to feel like this? You think I like waking up every day wondering if I'm still useful? If I'm still a man?"

Her voice cracked. "I think you're scared. And I think you're trying to drown it out instead of working through it."

They stared at each other in the dim light, the silence between them louder than any argument.

"I don't want to leave," she said finally. "I don't want to leave this house, this place. But I'm a bit lost, too."

Jack looked away. "Welcome to the club."

"I just don't know," she said. "But I do know I love you and I want you to believe in yourself again."

They didn't speak much the rest of the night, but the air between them had shifted—less anger, more sadness. They both knew the truth: they couldn't afford to stay. Not financially. Not emotionally. And so they committed to the decision. It wasn't easy. It wasn't joyful. But it was necessary.

They listed the house. Packed up their lives. Said goodbye to neighbors and friends. Elena cried when they took down the wind chimes from the porch. Jack stood in the empty living room the night before the movers came, staring at the walls as if they might speak to him. Perhaps saying, "Don't leave, you belong here."

"This was supposed to be our forever home," Elena whispered.

Jack took her hand. "Maybe Fort Worth is just the next chapter. Not the last one."

Jack went to a support group meeting the next day. He was quiet, listening most of the time. Toward the end he spoke up: "I just want to share that Elena and I are moving to Fort Worth, Texas," he said. "I accepted a job offer there. It was a tough decision, but with no opportunities turning up here, we had to take it."

The circle was quiet. Some people nodded, with looks of

understanding.

Malik spoke up. "You'll be missed," he said. "Thank you for being here."

Jack stood and shook hands with everyone. He thanked each person for their time and for sharing their story. Walking to his truck, he thought about the first meeting he attended, his hesitation and how that had transitioned into comfort, a safe place he could open share. A place of no judgement, just acceptance.

Two days later, Elena and Jack left California.

The drive along I-40 was long and quiet and very familiar to Jack. He couldn't help but think back to the long, somber drive away from Texas when he was a young boy. How could a drive in the opposite direction make him feel almost the same?

They took turns behind the wheel, the car packed with essentials, the rest of their belongings on some semi. Jack watched the landscape change, from coastal hills to dry valleys, to the high desert, and finally to the wide, flat plains of Texas.

On their way in, they stopped in Wellington to visit the grave sites of his mom, grandma, and grandpa. They did their best to clean them up and remove some weeds, then placed flowers at each of them.

Jack walked over to the rodeo grounds of his childhood dreams. The feel and smell of the dirt brought back a rush of memories. He climbed up on a chute door and just sat there for a while. He watched Claire run around smelling everything, occasionally running back to them, then running off to sniff another spot.

Elena leaned up against the door beside him. "If these grounds could talk, I bet they'd share some funny tales about a wild-haired little cowboy."

He laughed. "Being a kid here was the best." He tried to say more, but the emotions and nostalgia of it all were falling upon him, and that was all he could get out. He thought about all the places he'd lived. All the places he'd left.

And something clicked into place.

This time felt different. Not a deployment. Not an escape. A beginning. "We're going to be alright, babe. As long as we have each other."

Elena reached up to the chute and hugged his leg tight. Then, they made their way back to the car, took a lap around the town, and got back on the road.

Fort Worth was hot. The kind of heat that created heat waves rippling on the sidewalks. But the city was also welcoming and familiar, somehow. And the pace of life was slower.

The University of North Texas campus was sprawling and green. Jack's office was modest but bright, with a window that overlooked a courtyard filled with oak trees. His team was small but passionate, like him. People who understood how to help others.

On his first day, he stood in front of the senior executive cabinet members and introduced himself. For a moment, he panicked. *What am I doing here? I don't belong with these doctors and senior leaders.* But he looked around the room and reminded himself that these were just people, like him. He felt good.

"My name is Jack Mercer," he said. "I served 22 years in the Army. I've worked with organizations to help them improve. To build the right processes. And I'm here to help you do the same."

He saw heads nod. Eyes trying to read him.

He felt something shift inside him. Was it purpose?

That night, he and Elena sat on the porch of their friend's house, a modest brick home in a quiet neighborhood. The cicadas buzzed in the trees. The air smelled like freshly cut grass and barbecue.

"It's not Marin," she said.

"No," Jack said. "But it's not Iraq."

They gently laughed. She leaned her head on his shoulder, and it felt like home.

13
ELENA'S WAY

Elena was born in Flint, Michigan, in the heart of winter, February 1970. The snow was piled high that year, and the cold of the Northern winters seemed to settle into everything—rooftops, roads, and even the bones of the city. But Elena came into the world with fire in her spirit. From the beginning, she was inquisitive, bold, and unafraid to get her hands dirty.

She grew up in Durand, a small railroad town just a short drive from Flint, where the trains rumbled through and everyone knew everyone else's business. Elena was a tough little girl, the kind who scraped her knees and didn't cry, who climbed trees higher than the boys dared, and who played tackle football in the empty lot behind the gas station.

A never-ending source of fun could be found not far from her house: the town dump. The "off-limits" sign was merely a suggestion, and the dump felt full of mystery. Elena was drawn to it like a moth to a flame. She and her brother would explore it like archaeologists, digging through discarded treasures and building forts out of old pallets. In the winter, Elena and her friends would build more forts, out of snow, and tunnels in the snowplow berms.

When she was eight, Elena's world shifted.

One evening, they all sat in the living room, the TV off, the air heavy. Elena remembered the way her mom sat on the edge of the couch, hands folded tightly in her lap, eyes flicking between Elena and her older brother.

"I need to talk to you both," her mom said gently, her voice trembling just enough for Elena to notice. "I'm going to be moving out."

Elena blinked. "Where are you going?"

Her mom hesitated. "Not far. Just ... to a different place in town. Your dad and I, we've decided it's better this way."

Her brother looked confused, but Elena just stared at her mom, trying to make sense of the words. "Are we going with you?"

Her mom glanced at her dad, who sat in his recliner, arms crossed. "No more questions. You're going to stay here. With your dad."

Elena wanted to ask why, but she knew not to press.

Her mom looked at Elena and her brother, both of them with solemn expressions on their faces. "This is what's best. Your dad's going to take good care of you. And I'll still see you."

Elena didn't cry. No fits thrown. She just nodded, even though she didn't really understand. She looked over at her dad, who gave her a small, reassuring nod. "We'll be alright," he said simply.

Her parents separated quietly, without drama or shouting. There were no slammed doors or raised voices, just a stillness that settled over the house like dust. Her parents had agreed that her father would raise the kids. There was no custody battle, no courtrooms. Just a quiet understanding between two people who had grown apart.

It wasn't something Elena questioned at the time. She didn't have the words for it, and no one offered more than what was necessary. There were, in many ways, no changes to Elena's world. School, friends, bikes, snowball fights in winter. Her mom became an occasional visitor, loving but distant, never fully present, no longer a part of the daily rhythm.

Her dad was steady. A man of few words and a strong work ethic. He worked long hours at the school district, came home tired but was always there for them as a father. He made sure there was food on the table, heat in the house, and clean clothes in the drawers. He didn't talk much about feelings, but he showed up. Every day. And in his own quiet way, he did his best to keep things normal.

Elena learned early how to be strong. How to carry questions without answers. How to find comfort in routine, and resilience in silence. And though she didn't know it then, those early lessons would shape her into the woman she would become.

Elena missed her mom, of course, but she didn't dwell on it. She visited her a couple times at the apartment she had rented in town. Then, with no notice, Elena's mom moved to Arkansas. Once again, Elena didn't dwell on it. There were woods to explore, creeks to wade through, and friends to meet up with. It was never said aloud, but Elena was a daddy's girl. He had a hard time telling Elena no. She knew at a young age that being with her dad was the best option for her, and one she herself would have chosen.

Life kept rolling along. Summers were Elena's favorite. She'd pack a small suitcase and head to Rochester Hills, near Detroit, to stay with her cousins. They were older, cooler, and had closets full of clothes that Elena adored. She'd try on their hand-me-downs like they were runway pieces, twirling in front of the mirror and imagining a life beyond Durand. Those visits were filled with laughter, sleepovers, and whispered secrets under the covers. It was a different world, suburban, a bit more polished, and full of possibility.

By high school, Elena had begun to find her path. She was still tough, still the girl who didn't back down from a challenge, but she had also discovered a deep curiosity about the human body and how it worked. Science classes lit her up. Anatomy fascinated her. Her high school offered a course called Health Education Cluster, and she loved the idea of helping people, of being the one who could stay calm in chaos. The medical field called to her with a quiet drumbeat.

But college? That could wait.

She wasn't ready to sit in more classrooms. After years of textbooks, bells, and the same hallways, Elena felt like she was suffocating in routine. What she wanted, what she needed, was to see the world, to test herself, to break out of the small-town mold that had shaped her but never quite fit. So, she did something bold. Something no one in her circle expected.

She joined the Army.

Her friends didn't know what to make of it. "You're going to find yourself a big strong man in uniform," they teased, laughing as they made up stories. Elena just rolled her eyes. That was the last thing on her mind. She wanted life experience. She wanted college money. She wanted out.

But before she could sign anything, she knew she had to talk to her dad and get his approval.

It was the spring of her senior year in high school, on a cool Michigan evening, when she brought it up. They were sitting on the back porch, her dad nursing a cup of coffee, the sun dipping low behind the trees. The air smelled like fresh-cut grass and the faint smoke of someone grilling down the street.

"Dad," she said, her voice steady but quiet, "I've been thinking about what I want to do after graduation."

He looked over at her, one eyebrow raised. "Yeah? Thought you were leaning toward community college."

"I was," she said, "but I don't think I'm ready for more school. Not yet."

He nodded slowly, waiting.

"I want to join the Army," she said.

There was a pause. A long one. Her dad set his coffee down and leaned forward, elbows on his knees. "The Army?" he repeated, not with judgement, but with the weight of a father trying to understand.

"Yeah," she said. "I've been talking to a recruiter. I want to be a combat medic. It's medical training, it'll help pay for college later, and ... I just want to do something different. I want to see more than Durand."

He rubbed his chin, thoughtful. "You've always been tough. I'm not surprised you're thinking about something like this. But it's not easy, Elena. It's not just travel and adventure. It's hard work. It's sacrifice."

"I know," she said. "That's part of why I want to do it. I want to prove to myself that I can."

He looked at her for a long moment, his eyes softening. "You have the grit and tenacity for sure."

Elena blinked, listening to each word. "Yeah?"

"Yup. You're a force to reckon with, Elena."

He leaned back in his chair, sighing. "If this is what you want, I'll support you. Just promise me one thing."

"What's that?"

"Don't lose who you are in the process. The Army will shape you, sure, but don't let it take away that spark. That curiosity. That heart of yours."

Elena smiled, a lump rising in her throat. "I won't," she said. And she meant it.

She made two different trips to the Military Enlistment Processing Center. The first time they offered her something she didn't want, even though she made it clear that she only wanted to get into the medical field. The counselor said she didn't have a high enough score. So she stuck to her guns and walked out. She took time to study and retook the Armed Service Vocational Aptitude Battery a month later and knocked it out of the park.

On her second trip to the Military Enlistment Processing Center, the counselor questioned whether or not she herself took the ASVAB the second time, or if someone had taken it for her. They were surprised how much her score had improved.

"I studied!" she said in a demanding voice.

They had her take it again, to validate she truly studied, and she did just as well. Finally, she was in. She chose to become a combat medic, a role that combined her love of medicine with her desire to be in the thick of it.

Graduation came fast and summer went by even faster. Soon it was time for Elena to head out to basic training at Fort Dix, in New Jersey. She was excited and nervous, but ready. For many of the gals in her unit, basic training was a serious wake-up call, but not for Elena. She thrived. The inner warrior she'd always carried quietly came roaring to life. She loved the discipline, the physical challenge. She loved the rifle range and the grenade course. She wasn't just keeping up, she was leading.

After basic training, she was sent to Fort Sam Houston in San Antonio, Texas, for her medic training. Winter had arrived early back in Michigan, but in San Antonio, the sun was shining, and the air was a perfect 70 degrees. Elena felt like she had landed on another planet. Blue sky, warm weather, and no snow in sight.

She excelled in her training at Fort Sam Houston, rising quickly through the ranks of her class with a quiet confidence that surprised even her. While others stayed up late poring over anatomy flashcards and fumbling through trauma simulations, Elena absorbed the material like a sponge. The names of bones, the functions of organs, the protocols for triage and field care, it all clicked. It was as if the knowledge had always been there, waiting to be unlocked.

On her headphones, Modern English's "After the Snow" played over and over again as she easily memorized facts. In the trauma bay simulations, where chaos was simulated with flashing lights and shouting instructors, Elena stayed calm. Her hands were steady, her voice clear. She could assess and dress a wound and call out vitals with the precision of someone who had been doing it for years. Her instructors took notice. They didn't shower her with praise—this was the Army, after all—but they nodded more often when she spoke, called on her to demonstrate procedures, and paired struggling students with her during drills.

By the end of the course, she was tied for the top of her class. No fanfare, no ceremony, just her name on a list, and a few quiet nods of respect from instructors who didn't hand those out lightly. Her peers admired her, too, not just for her skill, but for her grit and easygoing personality. She wasn't the loudest or the flashiest, but she was the one you wanted next to you when things got real.

Elena had found her footing, not just in the Army, but in herself. She had left Durand behind, but the determination and resilience she'd grown up with were still there, woven into every step she took. The girl who once built forts in snowplow berms and played football behind the gas station had become a soldier, a medic. She had no idea yet, but her path would soon cross with someone else who had taken the challenging road toward finding purpose and exploring what life had to offer. A man named Jack.

14
FREE FALLING

Germany, 1990

The first time Jack noticed Elena, they were sitting on opposite sides of a classroom in a converted barracks building on a small U.S. Army base near Mainz. It was an evening college course, Intro to Earth Science, taught by a civilian professor who looked like she'd rather be anywhere else. Jack had enrolled mostly to keep his promotion packet competitive, showcasing his qualifications, performance, and readiness for increased responsibility and rank. Elena, he would later learn, was there because she genuinely liked learning.

They didn't speak that first night. Or the second. But he noticed her, with her golden hair pulled into a tight bun, her sharp eyes that scanned the room like she was always assessing, always keenly aware of everything around her. She laughed once at something the professor said, and Jack remembered thinking it was the first real sound he'd heard all day.

They saw each other around the base now and then, at the small PX, in the chow hall, passing in the motor pool. Always a nod, a glance, small talk, but never more.

Until the night at the club.

It was a Friday, and Jack had gone out with a friend from his unit. His buddy needed a wingman to occupy a friend of a girl he was planning to meet up with. Jack was hesitant.

"Dude," he groaned. "Ask Graham. I'm tired." It had been a long week for Jack with training, and his vehicle had a lot of scheduled maintenance that took up most of his week.

Sam was persistent. Like a damn yapping chihuahua.

The club was off post, tucked into a side street in the nearby village of Ingelheim. It was the club people went to when it was close to the end of the month, just before payday. Cheap drinks, dim lights, sticky floors, and a DJ who leaned heavily toward American rock and country. Jack was nursing a beer, half-listening to his buddy talk about a girl he was waiting for, when he saw her.

Elena.

She was standing near the bar with a couple of friends, wearing jeans and a white shirt, her hair down for once. She looked different. Softer. But still sharp.

Their eyes met.

She hesitated, then walked over.

"You're in my class," she said.

Jack nodded. "Yeah. I'm Jack."

"Elena."

There was a pause. Then she said, "Wanna dance?"

He blinked. "Sure."

The song changed. Tom Petty's "Free Fallin'" drifted through the speakers, slow and aching. They moved together, awkward at first, then easier. Jack wasn't much of a dancer, but Elena didn't seem to care. She smiled at him, and something in his chest shifted.

The song seemed to last forever. She gently rested her head on his chest.

What happened next has two different stories. His and hers.

His: He felt her lips lightly kiss his neck and he turned his head down to meet her kiss.

Hers: She gently brushed her face against his shoulder, and he turned to kiss her.

Her lips were soft. Kissing her felt right.

Either way, it was the beginning.

They started spending time together, drinks after class, walks through the village, and weekend trips to nearby towns. They explored castles and cathedrals, drank cheap wine by the Rhine, and got lost in cities, neither of them speaking the language very well. They laughed a lot.

Talked about everything and nothing.

One afternoon, they found an orchard just down the road from base. Rows of apple trees, the grass tall and golden. They lay beneath the branches, the sun warm on their faces, the world quiet for once.

That was the first time they made love.

It wasn't planned. But it was real and beautiful.

On weekends, they'd take the train to nearby villages, places with cobblestone streets, timber-framed houses, and bakeries that smelled deliciously of butter and cinnamon. Elena had a way of finding the quiet corners of every town, the hidden bookstores, the tucked-away beer gardens, the old churches with bells that rang like they were calling out to something ancient.

They wandered through Rothenburg ob der Tauber like they were in a fairy tale, holding hands beneath ivy-covered archways and laughing over mugs of glühwein. In Munich, they got lost in the crowds during Oktoberfest. It was overwhelming for Jack, but Elena stayed close to him, grounding him with a squeeze of her hand and a knowing smile. She always seemed to know when he needed a moment, even then, when the world got too loud.

Sometimes they'd rent a car and drive with no destination in mind, just following the winding roads through the Black Forest or along the Rhine. They'd stop when something caught their eye—a vineyard, a castle ruin, a roadside stand selling fresh cherries. Jack found something freeing in those aimless days. Elena brought out a softness in him, a curiosity he hadn't realized he still had. She rekindled his desire to see more places, explore different countries, and create memories.

At night, they talked about what comes next. About what they were afraid of. About what they hoped for.

They dated for two years, through field exercises, long shifts, and the constant churning of Army life. They fought sometimes, about time, about distance, about the future. But they always came back to each other.

They got married in October of 1992 at Fort Carson, Colorado. A small ceremony. A few family members and friends. Elena wore a beautiful dress. Jack wore a rented tux. They said their vows in a little chapel on post. There was a reception at the Officer's Club. It didn't seem real. Growing up, he had never imagined getting married. Maybe it wasn't something wild little boys did.

A quick and simple honeymoon, and it was back to reality.

Then came the moves. The deployments. The long nights apart.

And the children.

Their first daughter, Lily, was born in May of 1994. Jack held her in his arms and felt something crack open inside him. A kind of love he didn't know he was capable of. Elena was radiant, exhausted, and stronger than he'd ever seen her.

Lily was a handful as a baby. Colicky and always on the move. But when she was taken outside, she would just look up at the trees and sky. It was soothing for her.

Their second daughter, Ava, came in June of 1997. Jack almost missed the birth; he was deployed, able to come home quickly, and then had to leave shortly after. Elena didn't hold it against him. She sent photos, letters, and cassette tapes with the baby's coos and her own voice reading bedtime stories.

Their third and final daughter, Sophie, arrived in January of 2000. Jack made it home just in time after completing another military school. He cried when he saw her. Elena did, too.

Three girls. Three pieces of his heart walking around outside his body.

Elena was the anchor. The constant. She raised their daughters with fierce grace, even when Jack was gone months at a time. Even when he came home angry, withdrawn, distant.

He didn't know what was happening to him then. The rage. The numbness. The nightmares. He thought it was just stress. Just the job. He would shrug it off. "It comes with the work," he'd say.

But Elena knew it was something more. Something was wrong. She never said it outright. Never accused. But she saw him. The way he flinched at loud noises. The way he stared at nothing. The way he drank too much and apologized after the fact, only to do it again and again.

And still, she loved him.

There were more good years than bad. Laughter. Vacations. Christmas mornings with wrapping paper everywhere and three little girls squealing with joy. There were nights on the porch, just the two of them, watching the stars and talking about where they'd go when Army life was behind them.

But there were hard years, too. Jack's temper. His silence. The way he sometimes looked at her like he didn't recognize her or himself.

She carried more than her share. She was a mother, father, nurse, teacher, counselor. Sometimes she held the family together with sheer will.

And Jack, even in his worst moments, knew he didn't deserve her. In his moments of distress, he'd ask her, "Why do you stay with me? You deserve better."

"I love you. We're in this together, Jack," she would reply.

Looking back, he didn't know how she did it. How she held the family together while he unraveled. How she loved him through the worst of it. Maybe it was because she'd seen the best of him, too.

The man who danced with her to Tom Petty in a smoky German club.

The man who kissed her under the apple trees.

The man who, even broken, never stopped trying.

15
THE MAZE

It was just another morning. Clean up. Coffee. Then off to work. Jack had been working at the University of North Texas Health Science Center for almost a year now. They had settled in and found a house. Made it their own and took time for road trips. Claire enjoyed the backyard, chasing squirrels, and exploring Texas.

Jack left the house just after 6:30 a.m., coffee in a travel mug, his work bag slung over his shoulder. The Texas sky was still dark, the horizon just beginning to glow with the promise of sunrise. He kissed Elena goodbye, told her he'd see her that evening, and climbed into his truck.

He merged onto I-35, the highway already humming with early commuters and long-haul trucks. He turned on the stereo, connected it to his playlist, and settled into the rhythm of the road. His mind wandered to the day ahead: meetings, emails, maybe lunch with one of the student veterans. Just another Tuesday.

He never saw the semi.

The truck came barreling down the on-ramp too fast, its trailer swaying like a tail out of control. Jack caught a blur of motion in his peripheral vision, a flash of chrome and white, and then ... impact.

The sound was ear-shattering. Metal on metal. Glass exploding. Tires screaming. Jack's truck spun violently, then flipped. Once. Twice. Three times. It tumbled down an embankment, crashing through brush and dirt, and finally landed on its side in a shallow ravine.

Silence.

He was unconscious when the paramedics arrived. Barely breathing.

They cut him from the wreckage. His legs were mangled. His ribs shattered. His collarbone snapped like a dry twig. There was internal bleeding. A severe head injury. He flatlined once in the ambulance. Again in the ER.

The doctors placed him in a medically induced coma. They didn't know if he'd wake up.

Elena was at the hospital within the hour. She didn't leave. She slept in a chair beside his bed, her hand wrapped around his. She talked to him, even when he couldn't respond, repeating stories of special moments they shared. She read one of his favorite books to him, *Border Music*, by Robert James Waller. She played his favorite music: U2, Head and Heart, and Chris LeDoux. She told him stories about the girls, about their life, about the first time they danced to "Free Fallin'".

Late one night, when the hospital wing had gone quiet and while the machines beside Jack's bed beeped in steady rhythm, Elena folded her hands in her lap and bowed her head. She hadn't prayed in earnest in years, not since the girls were little and Jack was deployed in places she couldn't pronounce, but now, with her husband broken and unmoving, she found herself whispering into the silence.

"Please," she said, voice trembling. "Please don't take him. Not like this. Not now." Her tears fell freely, soaking into the blanket she clutched. "He's been through so much. He's still fighting. Just ... just let him come back to us." She stayed like that for a long time, eyes closed, heart open, hoping someone, anyone was listening.

Their daughters arrived—Lily from Cleveland, Ava from Austin, and Sophie from college in southern California. They took turns sitting with him, whispering memories, begging him to come back, and giving Elena small breaks, forcing her to take a walk, get some fresh air.

Jack's sister, Elizabeth, also flew in from California. And his brother, Michael, called every day.

The room was filled with love. And fear. Nurses constantly checked in, took time to listen, to talk, to give hope.

Jack didn't remember the accident. Not really. Just flashes. The sound of twisting metal. The sensation of falling. Then nothing.

But in the coma, something else happened.

He dreamed.

He dreamed he was in a maze.

The walls were high and made of stone, covered in moss and draped in shadows. The sky above was grey, the air thick with a dark layer of fog. He wandered, barefoot, confused. Every turn led to another dead-end. Trying to trace his steps back only led to more impasses. Every path looked the same. The walls all looked the same.

But he wasn't alone.

There were voices, soft and distant. People calling his name. Sometimes he saw shapes in the mist, shadows moving across the walls. Figures. Faces. Some seemed familiar. Others were not. They didn't speak. They just watched. He would try to run to them, only to have each one disappear.

He kept walking.

Sometimes he ran. Sometimes he fell. The maze shifted around him, like it was alive. He was exhausted. Lost. Afraid.

Then he saw them.

Two men.

They stood at a fork in the path, dressed in desert fatigues, stained and dirty. One was tall and thin, the other shorter, stockier. Their faces were smudged with ash and dirt, but each one looked calm. Familiar.

He stopped.

It took him a moment to recognize them.

The two Iraqi soldiers. The ones from the bunker. Desert Storm. His first firefight.

They didn't speak. They just nodded, then turned and began walking. Jack followed.

They led him through the maze, turn after turn, corridor after corridor. The fog began to lift. The walls grew lower. The sky brightened.

He didn't know why they were helping him. He didn't understand.

"Where are we going?" Jack asked. Neither replied. It felt like days passed as they kept walking along the stone path. Stopping at night to rest. Never speaking. At night the sky was filled with stars. The stars always seemed to be moving, and at times, Jack felt like he could reach out and touch them.

One night by a still river, they stopped to rest. Jack walked to the water. It was moving, but somehow also still as a mirror. He could hear it trickling over rocks. He looked down at the surface, to see his reflection, to see if he was even real. The reflection was there, it was him, but all around him he saw faint images of people circling. He couldn't make out any of their faces; they were blurry. But he sensed they were a part of him.

As morning came, the light warmed his body. He sat up from a bed of tall, soft grass. The soldiers were standing by the stone path. They nodded for him to come. The journey had to continue.

They led him deeper into the maze, their footsteps silent on the damp stone. Jack followed, unsure why, but certain he had no other choice. The air grew warmer as they walked, the fog thinning just enough for him to see the path ahead. The walls, once jagged and cold, began to smooth, as if worn down by time or memory.

The two men continued to say no words, but their presence was steady, grounding. Jack felt no fear from them, only a strange, quiet understanding. He wanted to ask them why they were here, why they were helping him, but every time he opened his mouth, no sound came out. Still, they seemed to know. They would glance back at him now and then, nodding gently, as if to say, keep going. You're almost there.

At one point, the path opened into a wide clearing. In the center stood a mirror, tall and freestanding, its surface rippling like water. Jack stepped toward it and saw himself, not as he was now, broken and bruised, but as he had once been—young, in uniform, a rifle slung over his shoulder, eyes sharp and full of fire. Behind him shadows flickered, faces of men he'd served with, some smiling, some solemn, some gone.

He turned to the two men. They stood on either side of the mirror, watching him. One had his hand over his heart, and the other raised a hand and pointed toward the reflection. Jack stepped forward, touched the glass, and it gave way like mist.

He fell through. He fell for what felt like entire days. Then he landed in tall grass. Nothing else around. Only tall green grass and blue skies as far as he could see. He started walking. He began to hear strange noises, the distant chatter of people, and bright lights that made it hard to see.

He woke on the fourteenth day.

Jack's eyes began to blink open, the return was slow—like surfacing from deep underwater. The room was blurry, the lights too bright, the sounds distant and muffled. He couldn't move, couldn't speak, but he was awake. Alive. Elena had been dozing in the chair beside him, her hand still wrapped around his. When she felt the twitch of his fingers, she looked up and froze. "Jack?" she whispered, leaning in.

His eyes met hers. She gasped, then screamed for the doctors, her voice cracking with disbelief and joy. "He's awake! He's awake!" The room erupted in motion, nurses rushing in, monitors beeping faster, a doctor calling for vitals. But all Jack could see was Elena's face, streaked with tears, her hand trembling as she touched his cheek. "You came back," she whispered. "You came back to me."

He spent another three weeks in the hospital. Surgeries. Endless tests. He couldn't walk. He could barely sit up. But he was alive.

The doctors called it a miracle.

He called it something else.

He didn't tell anyone about the maze. Or the two men. Not at first. It felt too strange. Too sacred. But it stayed with him, clearer than any dream he'd ever had. He didn't know what it meant. But he did know this: he wasn't done. He had been spared. Given life, when death should have prevailed.

Before they wheeled him out upon discharge, two officers had stopped by his room, their voices low but firm as they laid out glossy photos of twisted metal and shattered glass. Jack stared at the wreckage, trying to reconcile the mangled frame with the memory of his truck. "Do you remember anything?" one asked. He shook his head, throat dry. The other officer tapped the photo, eyes narrowing. "You shouldn't be alive after that wreck," he said quietly. "You must have had angels protecting you."

The words lingered as the wheelchair bumped over the curb, pulling him backward in time, to heat shimmering off endless sand, the smell of dust and diesel. The Bedouin elder, his face carved by sun and wind, sharing in broken English, "You have angels protecting you." Back then, Jack had laughed it off. Now, he wasn't sure.

It was strange leaving the hospital grounds in his wheelchair; it felt like stepping into a different world. The city was louder than he remembered, cars honking, people rushing past, conversations merging together like static.

Driving home, Jack was in deep thought, looking over the images from the wreck in his mind and contemplating what the police officer said. Elena looked over at him and placed her hand on his thigh. "What's on your mind, babe?"

He hesitated. It all sounded a bit unreal, the stuff of Sci-Fi books. But he knew Elena wouldn't judge or jump to conclusions. Jack shifted in his seat, his voice low as if sharing a secret. "When the police showed me those pictures …they said I shouldn't be alive, that I must have angels protecting me." He paused, eyes distant. "And for a second, I was back in the desert. There was this old Bedouin man. He told me the same thing. 'You have angels protecting you.' I thought it was just talk. But now …" His words trailed off.

Elena smiled, soft and steady, like sunlight breaking through clouds. She reached for his hand and said gently, "I wouldn't doubt it."

Jack spent weeks in his wheelchair. It was an annoyance he disliked more with each new outing. No matter how carefully Elena had planned and prepared for an excursion, whether a short trip to a nearby café or a visit to the hospital, Jack felt out of place.

He traversed uneven sidewalks, every crack sending a jolt through his arms as he maneuvered the wheels. But what Jack didn't realize was that each trip was monumental. It meant progress.

Yet, people stared. Some looked away quickly, seemingly embarrassed. Others didn't bother hiding their curiosity. Jack hated it. He hated the way the chair made him feel small, how it turned him into something to be pitied or ignored.

Inside restaurants, the tables were too close together, and he had to ask someone to move so he could pass. Elena handled it all with grace—smiling, chatting, making it seem normal. But Jack felt the heat rise in his face. He couldn't shake the feeling that he didn't belong here anymore, not in this body, not in this world.

One outing, when his coffee came, he couldn't even lift the cup without his hand shaking. Elena reached over, steadying it without a word. That small gesture, so gentle, so unspoken, cut through the noise. He looked at her, and for a moment, the world quieted. Maybe he wasn't ready to face the world or the rest of his life. But he wasn't alone.

16
THE OTHER SIDE

Basra, Iraq. February 1991

Their names were Hassan and Majid.

They were not soldiers by choice. Only simple and hard-working villagers in Balad Ruz.

Hassan was a schoolteacher. He taught Arabic literature to teenagers in a dusty classroom with broken windows and a chalkboard that hadn't been replaced in years. He loved poetry, especially the old verses of Al-Mutanabbi, and he often recited them to his daughter at bedtime. He had a wife, Layla, and another child too—his pride and joy, a boy named Omar, who had just turned three.

Majid was a mechanic. He worked in his uncle's garage, fixing Soviet-era trucks and rusted-out cars. He was quiet, thoughtful, and had a laugh that came from deep in his chest. He had married young, to a woman named Samira, and they had one child, a daughter named Noor, who loved to braid his hair when he came home from work.

They were friends. Neighbors. Fathers. Men who wanted nothing more than to live quietly and raise their children in peace.

But peace was not an option.

Hassan and Majid had watched the invasion of Kuwait unfold with a mixture of disbelief and dread. Neither of them supported the war. How could they? It wasn't their fight. They had no interest in oil fields or political posturing. They were men of modest means, trying to raise families in a country that had long since stopped caring about its people. They spoke quietly, behind closed doors, about how reckless and dangerous Saddam's government had become. They feared the secret police, the informants, the way neighbors disappeared overnight. But more than anything, they feared what would come next.

"This will bring fire to our doorstep," Majid had said one night, his voice low. Hassan nodded, staring out the window. "And we'll be the ones burned."

When Iraq invaded Kuwait, it came fast and without mercy. The Iraqi government, knowing an allied response was imminent, was desperate for soldiers, and began conscripting men from every corner of the country. Police and military officers went door to door. Refusal meant prison. Or worse, retaliation against your family.

Hassan and Majid were taken on the same day. No time for goodbyes, no kisses, no hugs. No time to look into their wives' eyes and say, "I love you." The soldiers grabbed them by the arms and yelled commands to get on the truck.

They didn't want to fight. They didn't want to die. Many of the new soldiers were young—barely out of their teens—wearing uniforms that didn't quite fit and carrying weapons they barely understood. Their hands trembled not from the weight of the rifles, but from the crushing uncertainty of what lay ahead. They were afraid—terrified, really. Not just of the Americans, whose firepower and precision were unlike anything they'd ever imagined, but of their own regime. Of the brutal consequences that came with disobedience. Of the whispered stories of soldiers who had tried to run and were never seen again.

Hassan and Majid were sent south, toward the Kuwaiti border, to man a bunker that had already been shelled half to rubble.

They feared for their families. For their mothers and sisters and children who would bear the punishment if they deserted. The regime didn't just punish the soldier—it punished the bloodline. That fear was a leash, tight and unforgiving. So they stayed. They would fight. Not out of loyalty, but out of desperation. Out of a belief that maybe, just maybe, making it through one more day would bring something different. Each day they prayed quietly, lips moving in trembling rhythm.

On the morning of February 24th, they heard the rumble before they saw anything. The ground shook. The sky grew darker, filled with dust. The American forces were coming. Tanks, armored vehicles, helicopters overhead. A storm of steel and fire.

Hassan clutched his rifle with trembling hands. Majid sat beside him, eyes wide, lips moving in silent prayer.

"What do we do?" Hassan whispered.

Majid shook his head. "I don't know."

They looked at each other. Two men caught in a war they didn't start, wearing uniforms that didn't belong to them.

They didn't want to shoot. They didn't want to kill. But they were terrified.

So, they fired.

Not at the enemy. Not at anyone.

They raised their rifles and fired into the air—wild, panicked bursts. A signal. A cry. A desperate attempt to say, *We're here. We're scared. We don't want this.*

When they stopped firing, everything was still for a moment.

And then bursts of bullets shredded the air around them and they died quickly, easily. Hassan was thrown backward, his head striking the bunker wall. Majid fell beside him, his chest torn open. Explosions followed, but the men never heard them. A grenade, or maybe a shell. The bunker shook.

They died within seconds. No last words. No goodbyes.

Just silence.

As the U.S. forces went by, one vehicle stopped, looming over the bunker. Then it slowly continued on its path forward.

Majid's daughter, Noor, was turning five in a couple days.

Hassan had plans to visit his brother in Turkey.

Their families would not know their fate for over a month. No news. No information from the military. Their bodies were found by more American soldiers hours later, the secondary units following the path of destruction. One of the dead men was still clutching his rifle. The other had his eyes open, staring at the sky.

To the American soldiers, they were just two more enemy combatants. Two more threats neutralized.

But they were more than that.

They were fathers. Husbands. Friends.

They were men who had once danced at weddings, who had held their children close, who had laughed over tea in the evenings.

They were men who didn't want to die.

Years later, in a coma, Jack Mercer would see them again.

Not as enemies, though. As guides.

They stood in the maze with him, silent and steady, leading him through the fog. They didn't speak. They didn't accuse. They simply walked beside him, showing him the way out.

And when Jack woke, he remembered their faces, not as they were in death, but as they were in life.

17
THE HEALER

Omar Hassan Al-Karim had barely known his father. All he had were fragmented, distant memories and tales told by old photographs

He had been only three years old when his father, Hassan, was conscripted into the Iraqi Army and sent south to the Kuwaiti border. His mother, Layla, never spoke about the war. She only said that Hassan hadn't wanted to go. And that he had kissed Omar's forehead the night before he left and whispered, "Be better than me."

For years, Omar carried his father's absence like an open wound. He was angry at the war, at the government, and at the world. Angry at the Americans who had invaded, and angry at the regime that had sent his father to die. He didn't know who to blame, so he blamed everyone.

But time had a way of softening even the sharpest edges.

Omar was a gifted student. Quiet, observant, always asking questions. His mother encouraged him to study, to read, to dream beyond the dust and rubble of post-war Iraq. When he was 16, he earned a scholarship through an international education program. It was a long shot, but he was accepted.

And so he moved to the United States in 2006.

Cleveland, Ohio was cold. Brutally cold. The snow shocked him at first, the way it blanketed everything, the way it silenced the world. It was nothing like Basra. But he adapted. He learned to layer his clothes, to drink hot coffee, and to walk carefully on icy sidewalks.

He was accepted into Case Western Reserve University, then medical school. He studied late into the night, driven by something deeper than ambition. He didn't just want to succeed. He wanted to heal. To give back. To make sense of the loss that had shaped his life.

He knew his father had died in the war. He didn't know how. For years, he imagined it had happened in explosive flashes, gunfire, smoke, on a nameless battlefield. He hated the thought of it. Hated that his father had been reduced to a statistic, a casualty, a footnote in someone else's war.

But as he grew older, something shifted. He began to understand that war didn't belong to one side. That pain wasn't exclusive. That the men who fought often had no choice.

He stopped being angry. He started listening, learning, and forgiving.

Nearing 40, Omar was a physician at the Cleveland Clinic. He specialized in vascular medicine. He worked on complex cases and rare conditions, the ones that required not only skill but deep patience and empathy. His patients loved him. His colleagues respected him. He was known for his calm demeanor, his quiet confidence, and his ability to sit with people in their pain without trying to fix it too quickly.

He took long walks in the parks after work, among the trees, along the frozen paths. It reminded him of something he couldn't quite name. Maybe peace. Maybe his father.

Sometimes, late at night, he would sit by his window and look out at the snow-covered street. He would think about the life his father might have lived. About the man he might have been.

And sometimes, in the quiet, he would whisper, "I'm trying, Baba. I'm trying to be better."

And in those moments, he felt close to him.

The anger had faded. Love took its place.

18
THE LONG ROAD BACK

Jack had faced pain before. He'd felt it in the heat of battle, in the cold silence of loss, and in the quiet moments between deployments when his body reminded him of every mile he'd marched and every fall he'd taken. But nothing compared to this.

The doctors had informed him that recovery would be long and grueling and that he would have to be patient. "Recovery will take time, Jack," they reiterated. "You've got a long road ahead of you, Jack."

Physical therapy started three days after he was discharged from the hospital. At first, it was simple, just sitting up in bed without passing out. But even that felt as hard as climbing a mountain. His muscles, once toughened by years of military life, had atrophied. His joints screamed in protest. Every movement was a reminder of what he'd lost.

The mornings always started early. Jack was wheeled into the rehab center just after sunrise, the sterile scent of antiseptic already thick in the air. The room was bright, too bright, with floor-to-ceiling windows that let in the kind of harsh sunlight that made everything feel exposed. His therapist, Marcus, was a former college athlete with a calm demeanor and a voice that didn't rise, even when Jack's temper did. The sessions began with stretches—slow, deliberate movements that felt like torture. Jack's stiff muscles resisted every motion. Sweat beaded on his forehead before they even got to the parallel bars. The bars were the real test. Standing between them, gripping the cold metal, Jack would try to shift his weight forward, coaxing his legs to remember what they once did without thought. Every step was a negotiation between pain and willpower. Elena sat nearby, notebook in hand, offering quiet encouragement. Sometimes she read to him while he worked, passages from books they used to love, or articles she thought might make him laugh. He didn't always respond, but her voice grounded him. By the end of the hour, Jack was exhausted, his shirt soaked, his hands trembling. But he had moved. He had fought. That counted.

The medications were supposed to help. They dulled the pain, but they also dulled everything else. Nausea became a constant companion. He couldn't eat, couldn't sleep, and couldn't think straight. The pills made him feel like a ghost in his own skin. Eventually, he started refusing them. He chose the pain instead. At least it was real.

Each day in therapy was a war of inches. Standing up. Taking a step. Lifting his arm. Tasks that once came without thought now required every ounce of his focus and grit. The therapists were kind but relentless. They pushed him, and he pushed back, sometimes in silence, sometimes with rage. But he never quit.

Now, Jack sat on the padded bench, sweat clinging to his brow, his breath still ragged from the last set of exercises. Marcus, his physical therapist, crouched beside him, clipboard in hand but eyes focused, not on the notes, but on Jack himself.

"You're doing better than you think," Marcus said, his voice calm, steady. He was young, mid-20s, maybe, but there was a gravity to him that made Jack listen. Marcus had once been a star wide receiver in college, destined for the NFL until a torn ACL during his junior year shattered that dream.

"I know what it's like," he continued, "to have your body betray you. To wake up one day and realize the future you planned isn't going to happen."

Jack looked at him, surprised by the honesty. The gap in years between them was wide, but in that moment he felt like they were peers, two men who had been forced to rebuild.

"But I found something better," Marcus added, a small smile tugging at the corner of his mouth. "Helping people get back up. It's not the stadium, but it's real."

Jack nodded slowly, the weight of the conversation settling on him.

For the first time in a long while, he felt understood—not just as a patient, but as a man trying to find his footing again.

Then there was Elena.

She had been there from the beginning, quiet at first, hovering at the edge of the hospital room like a shadow. But as the days turned into weeks, she became his anchor. She learned the names of his nurses, memorized his medication schedule, and kept a notebook filled with questions for the doctors. She was his advocate when he was too tired to speak, his voice when he couldn't find the words.

But more than that, she was his strength.

When Jack couldn't lift himself out of bed, Elena was there, coaxing him with gentle encouragement and a firm hand on his back. When he lashed out in frustration, she didn't flinch. She listened. She stayed. She reminded him, without ever saying it, that he wasn't alone.

One morning, after a particularly brutal session, Jack collapsed into the wheelchair, drenched in sweat and shaking. He stared at the floor, jaw clenched, every muscle in his body trembling. Elena knelt beside him, her hand resting lightly on his knee.

"You're doing it," she said softly. "You're winning."

He didn't feel like he was winning. He felt broken. But her words stayed with him.

There were days when he wanted to give up. When the pain was too much, and the progress too slow. But Elena never let him spiral. She brought him books, music, and stories from the outside world. She made him laugh when he didn't think he could. She reminded him of who he was before the accident and who he could still become.

One night, long after visiting hours had ended, Jack woke to find her asleep in the chair beside his bed, her hand still wrapped around his. The room was dark and quiet except for the soft hum of machines. He looked at her, really looked, and something shifted inside him.

This wasn't just about healing his body. It was about reclaiming his life. For himself. For her.

He kept going.

He learned to walk again, one shaky step at a time. He learned to breathe through the pain, to find rhythm in the struggle. He learned to accept help—not through weakness, but as a form of strength. And through it all, Elena was there. Not to carry him, but to walk beside him.

There was a moment, months into his recovery, when he finally stood on his own, no cane, no brace, no hand to steady him. Just Jack. Elena stood across the room, tears in her eyes, pride written across her face.

"You did it," she whispered.

He nodded, breathless. "We did."

19
BASIC TRAINING

July 1989

Enlisting in the Army had been a spur-of-the-moment decision. Jack had never thought about serving in the military. He had family who had served during each of the World Wars and in Vietnam. Still, enlisting was something that hadn't crossed his mind. For quite a few years, he had planned to be a chef. Cooking with his grandma had ignited his passion for food, for making something from scratch into an incredible meal.

He had graduated high school and was waiting on starting college. He needed a break before he dove back into the books and classrooms. The structure of school, the deadlines, the noise, it all felt too close, too soon.

Jack needed time to get away, to a place he could be alone and amid almost unimaginable beauty. He went to the mountains.

He started taking solo trips to Echo Lake, nestled high in the Sierra Nevada, just beyond the winding switchbacks of Highway 50. The drive itself was a kind of meditation: windows down, pine-scented air rushing in, U2 and The Smiths humming low from the radio. He'd park near the trailhead, lace up his boots, and disappear beyond the granite landscape into the trees.

The hikes weren't about distance or speed. They were about stillness. About breathing. The trails around Echo Lake wound through granite outcroppings and alpine lakes, past glacial boulders and clusters of wildflowers that seemed to bloom just for him. As he climbed higher, past Echo Lake, he reached Lake Aloha. The lake was a mirror, so still in the early mornings that it reflected the bordering boulders, trees, and sky with perfect clarity. Jack would sit on a rock at the water's edge, watching the light shift across the surface, listening to the wind whisper through the air.

There were days he didn't see another soul. Just an occasional chipmunk darting across the trail or the distant call of a hawk overhead. He brought a small journal with him, jotting down thoughts, sketches, fragments of dreams. It was the first time in a long while he felt like he could hear himself think.

Those solo hikes gave him something he hadn't realized he was missing: peace. The kind that settles in your bones when you know you're exactly where you're supposed to be, even if just for a little while.

The instability at home hadn't lessened. As he matured, the discordance became more apparent. His mother's struggles continued. She'd have a stretch of sobriety, then a relapse; it was a continuous stream of chaos and uncertainty. His father remained a ghost, an unreliable figure that came and went in his thoughts, an absence that gnawed at him more profoundly than any tangible pain. Mostly it was the unanswered questions. *"How could he do this?" "Why doesn't he help?"* Jack's sister and brother were out on their own, creating lives, perhaps escaping, attempting to find their own peace. The familiar comfort of his bedroom, once a sanctuary and playground full of imaginary tales, had become a symbol of his limitations, a reminder of the life he felt trapped in.

One day he sat alone in his car after work. Not ready to drive home. Not wanting to head over to anyone's place to hang out. He was tired of what had become the norm. Drinking. People's bullshit. People pushing drugs. He knew it had to end. This was not the life he wanted. Even going to school wasn't going to help him get away. And that's what he wanted to do. Get away. Start fresh.

Jack drove home and didn't speak to anyone. His mom was asleep in her room, his stepdad watching television. He went to his room and grabbed his social security card, birth certificate, and high school diploma. Then he drove to the military recruiting center closest to him.

Once there, he parked and looked at the grey brick building. Not thinking too much, just staring. And then quietly, to himself, he said, "Let's go, Jack."

He walked into the building and briefly looked down the hall, scanning left to right. To his right a door was open, and he walked in.

Ten days later he was heading to basic training at Fort Sill, Oklahoma, with the U.S. Army. He told the recruiter he was ready to go. No issues. Nothing holding him back. That same night, he took the Armed Services Vocational Aptitude Battery and the next morning a physical. Then he selected a skill to be trained in, with a guaranteed first assignment to Germany. He only asked one question: "How quick can I leave?" That was June 30, 1989.

On July 10, 1989, he waited outside of his house for the recruiter to pick him up and take him to the Greyhound bus depot. Then it was on to the Oakland Military Entrance Processing Station for final processing. His family and the few friends who stopped by to say goodbye stood around. Most were still in shock.

"Is this really what you want, Jack?" his mom asked, as she held back tears.

Jack nodded and said, "I need this, Mom."

She understood what he meant and said nothing else.

When the recruiter arrived, Jack said his goodbyes, gave a few hugs, and kissed his mom on the cheek. "Love you, Mom. I'll write soon."

Then he got in the front seat and rode away.

When he arrived in Oakland, he walked to the MEPS building. They quickly processed him and put him in a shuttle with a dozen other new recruits. Off to airports in San Francisco, then Dallas, then he caught a puddle jumper to Lawton, Oklahoma, and finally a shuttle to Fort Sill's reception center. It was after midnight when he arrived.

A sergeant came out and took each person's packet and had them follow him inside to a large open bay area. He instructed them how to get into a formation. Then all of their bags were emptied and everything they had brought was gone through meticulously.

The only things Jack had brought were an address book, deodorant, a toothbrush, toothpaste, a change of clothes, and the small green bag everything was in.

"You're traveling light, boy," the sergeant said. "Running from something or someone?"

Jack wasn't sure of what to say or if he should say anything. "No, sir," he said in a mild tone.

A quick reply was barked out: "Boy! I work for a living. Call me sergeant."

Jack's first lesson learned. Sergeants work for a living.

It was almost three in the morning by the time he was shown to his temporary bunk. He didn't even bother making his bed. He took his shoes off, placed the neatly folded linen on the end of the bed, and lay down to sleep.

The first few days of in-processing were a blur of paperwork, vaccinations, uniforms being issued, and endless lectures on regulations and procedures. Then haircuts. They all stood in a single file line outside of the barber shop. There were guys with long hair, big hair, and wild curly hair like Jack's. As the guys went in, strangers came out, each with the same new haircut, skin-tight, as close to being bald as one could get. The haircuts were over quick—just step inside, sit down, and spin around. "Next!" they'd shout. If not for the rush to move from here to there, the moment would have been humorous, Jack thought, but this was neither the time nor place. The sheer volume of information to take in was staggering.

The Oklahoma heat in July was merciless. It invaded your lungs, soaked your clothes, and turned every breath into a chore. Fort Sill was a furnace, and basic training was the crucible.

Jack arrived at his basic training unit with a buzz cut, a duffel bag slung over his shoulder, and a quiet fire in his chest. He didn't know what to expect, only that he wasn't going to be the one who quit. They loaded up in an old cattle car, standing packed like sardines, each man holding on to a bar overhead. They headed to the other side of Fort Sill, across the tracks.

From the moment the bus doors opened, the shouting began. Drill sergeants descended on them like a storm, faces inches from theirs, with powerful, unrelenting voices. "Move! Faster! Eyes forward, you little maggot! You think this is a game?" There was no easing into it. Day one was a shock to the system, and it only got harder from there.

The days ran together in a haze of sweat, dirt, and adrenaline. Reveille at 0430. Formation by 0500. PT in the sweltering morning heat, with push-ups, sit-ups, rolling in the sand this way and then that way, sprints, and long-distance runs that left Jack gasping. The red Oklahoma clay clung to everything—boots, uniforms, skin. It got into their eyes, their mouths, their beds. It became part of them.

The weather was as much an enemy as the training. One day, the sun would beat down and roast them like a Thanksgiving turkey, the heat index soaring past 110 degrees. The next, a thunderstorm would roll in without warning, turning the training fields into rivers of mud. Jack remembered one afternoon on the obstacle course when the sky cracked open mid-climb. Rain poured in sheets, lightning forked across the sky, but the drill sergeants didn't flinch.

"You think the enemy's going to wait for sunshine, sweetheart?" they yelled.

So, the recruits kept going, soaked, shivering, slipping off ropes and walls slick with rain. Jack's hands bled from the rope burns, but he didn't stop. He had always considered himself to be in decent physical shape. But the constant ache of muscles he never knew existed and the agony of the never-ending push-ups told him otherwise.

Every day brought a new challenge. Weapons training, land navigation, forced marches with packs that felt heavier than they had any right to be. Classes in rooms that were designed to lull you to sleep. Jack's body screamed in protest. His calves cramped at night, his shoulders ached constantly, and his feet were a mess of blisters and calluses. But he kept pushing. He learned to embrace the discomfort, to find pride in the struggle. He wasn't the fastest or the loudest, but he was steady. Focused. Unbreakable.

The mental challenges were even more grueling. Sleep deprivation, coupled with relentless psychological pressure, created a state of constant fatigue. Decision-making became increasingly difficult, the recruits' minds clouded by exhaustion and stress. The drill sergeants seemed to delight in testing their limits, pushing them to the breaking point, prodding them with insults and ridicule. They were stripped of their identity, reduced to last names only—if you were lucky. The not-so-lucky got nicknames, another way to mentally break them down. Slowly each person's individuality was erased in a process designed to mold them into something more: obedient soldiers.

Jack was selected as the first of many rotating platoon leaders. His stint lasted a week. Longer than most. During that time, he never sat, was always in motion, taking directions from the drill sergeants and passing them on to the platoon. Exhaustion was his companion.

But he liked the structure. The predictability. Every minute of every day had a purpose. There was comfort in the routine, knowing that if he just kept moving, kept grinding, he would get through it. And he did more than get through it—he thrived. He shot expertly on the rifle range. He led his squad during field exercises. He earned the respect of his peers and the grudging approval of the drill sergeants, who started calling him "Old Man Jack" because of his quiet discipline and relentless drive.

As weeks turned into months, the exhaustion began to yield to a sense of accomplishment. The physical conditioning, once a source of unrelenting pain, became a source of pride. Jack learned to push himself beyond his perceived limits, to discover reserves of strength he never knew existed. His platoon mastered the art of teamwork, learning to rely on each other, to support each other, to train as one. Jack became more than friends with a few of his fellow soldiers. They had formed a brotherhood, pushing one another and listening to one another during long, tiring nights.

As time passed, the drill sergeants' demeanor slowly changed, from relentless driving and harsh language to almost a sort of cruise-control, speaking to the recruits as fellow soldiers, as part of a team. They shared experiences, answered questions about what could be expected moving forward. In those moments, Jack learned what being a part of the Army really meant.

Then, one day, it was over.

Graduation came with a strange mix of pride and disbelief. The same parade field they had marched across in silence now echoed with cheers and applause. Jack stood tall in his dress greens, shoes polished to a mirror shine, chest swelling as the commanding officer called his name. In the crowd, he spotted his mother, tears in her eyes, and his two uncles, both veterans themselves, standing with arms crossed and proud smiles. They had made the trip to see him become a soldier.

As the ceremony ended and the crowd spilled onto the field, Jack felt a hand on his shoulder. It was Drill Sergeant McCallister. "You did good, private," he said, his voice lower than usual. "You hung tough. That matters." Jack nodded, unsure of what to say. He didn't need to say anything. The look in the sergeant's eyes said enough.

Jack enjoyed a real meal after the ceremony with his family. It had been a while since he could just sit and slowly eat, enjoying each bite and having a conversation. He and his family laughed at the stories Jack shared. His uncles shared a few of their own and together they relived memories. His mom was glowing with pride.

That night, as the sun dipped below the horizon and the sky turned a deep, dusty orange, Jack sat alone on the barracks steps. The air was still hot, thick with the scent of sun-baked earth and distant diesel, but it felt different now—less oppressive, more alive. The wind stirred faintly, carrying with it the echoes of cadence calls and bootsteps, fading into the quiet.

He had come to Fort Sill with an open mind, unsure of what he was chasing—discipline, direction, maybe redemption. It was supposed to be just another step, a checkpoint on his road forward. But something had shifted. In the sweat, the drills, the silence between orders, he had begun to shed pieces of who he used to be. Not all at once, but in fragments—like armor falling away.

He stared out across the parade field, now empty and bathed in twilight, and felt the weight of everything he'd carried. His home life. His mother's scars. For the first time in a long while, he didn't feel crushed by life. He felt ready.

This wasn't just a step toward something more.

It was the beginning of something entirely new.

And Jack knew—deep in his bones—he was leaving a different man.

20
BENEATH THE SURFACE

Jack had learned to live with pain. He had accepted the slow grind of physical therapy, the stiffness in his joints, the fatigue that clung to him like a second skin. But this time it was different.

The pain in his abdomen started as a dull ache, easy to dismiss. At first, he thought it was just another side effect of the trauma his body had endured. But it grew. Some days it was a sharp, stabbing sensation that doubled him over without warning. Other times it was a deep, twisting pressure that made it hard to breathe, let alone move. It came in waves, unpredictable and unforgiving. Worst of all, no one could tell him why.

The VA sent him to specialist after specialist. Gastroenterologists, pain management doctors, even a neurologist. Each appointment ended the same way: a furrowed brow, a few scribbled notes, and the familiar refrain of "Let's run some more tests." Jack was losing count of the scans, the blood work, the poking and prodding. Every test came back inconclusive. Every answer led to more questions.

Jack's frustration boiled over. He wasn't just in pain, he was angry. Angry at the system, at the endless bureaucracy, at the feeling he was being passed around like a problem no one wanted to solve. He'd fought through war zones, survived an accident that should've killed him, and now he was being undone by something invisible. Something no one could name.

"What the hell am I even doing here?" Jack had yelled at the last appointment, another three hours of his day wasted.

Elena tried to stay strong, but Jack could see the worry in her eyes. She sat beside him at every appointment, took notes, asked questions the doctors didn't always want to answer. At night, when Jack couldn't sleep, he'd find her at the kitchen table, laptop open, scrolling through medical journals and veterans' forums. She was trying to piece together a puzzle that even the experts couldn't solve.

Then came the appointment at the Dallas VA.

The doctor was different—older, quieter, with a calm that felt earned. He listened more than he spoke, and asked questions that made Jack pause. After the exam, he checked to ensure the door was closed all the way. Then he locked it.

Jack and Elena exchanged a glance. The doctor sat down across from them, his voice low.

"I don't want to alarm you," he began, "but I've been reviewing your history, your symptoms, and the imaging we've done so far. From my research, all signs point to something called an aortic aneurysm."

Jack blinked. The words didn't register at first.

The only thing he could get out was, "What?"

"It's rare," the doctor continued, "but not unheard of, especially in men your age, particularly those with a history of physical trauma and high stress. It's a weakening in the wall of the aorta. If it ruptures ..." He didn't finish the sentence. He didn't have to.

Elena's hand found Jack's.

"It's only a possibility, a hunch you could say. Prior to working here, I worked at the Cleveland Clinic. We did a lot of research there and one of the studies was on aortic aneurysms." The doctor continued to explain that an aneurysm is essentially a bulge in the aorta, and can develop in two main areas: thoracic and abdominal.

The doctor's words hung in the air like smoke. Aortic aneurysm. Jack heard them, but they didn't quite land. He sat there, shoulders slumped, eyes fixed on a spot on the floor that didn't move. His mind was a blur of static. He'd come in expecting another round of vague theories and inconclusive tests, not this. Not something that was actually serious. Not something that could kill him. The room felt smaller, the air thinner.

Elena, on the other hand, snapped into focus. Her voice was calm but insistent as she leaned forward in her chair. "How big is it?" she asked. "Where exactly is it located? What kind of imaging do we need to confirm this? How soon can he see the specialist? Why hasn't this been identified earlier?" She fired off questions with the precision of someone who had spent too many nights researching worst-case scenarios.

The doctor answered each question carefully, respectfully, but Jack barely registered the exchange. He was still trying to process the idea that something inside him, something silent and hidden, might be waiting to tear him apart. He felt like a passenger in his own body, watching the conversation unfold from a distance, unable to speak, unable to move.

"I'll put in a referral for a vascular specialist," the doctor said. "Someone outside the VA system. This is more complicated than what we're equipped to handle here. I'm not saying this is definitely what's going on, but it needs to at least be ruled out. And we need to do it quickly."

Jack sat in stunned silence. The pain in his gut suddenly felt heavier, more real. Not just a symptom, but a dire warning.

As they left the office, the Texas sun was blazing overhead but Jack felt cold. The road ahead of him, already steep and treacherous, had just taken a darker turn. But he wasn't alone. Elena was beside him, her grip firm, her eyes fierce. Whatever came next, they would face it together.

The drive home was silent. The hum of the tires on the highway was the only sound. Jack stared out the passenger window, watching the Texas landscape blur past, flat fields already marked out for future slapped-together housing communities, traffic rushing by, the occasional road sign shimmering in the heat. His mind was still stuck in that exam room, replaying the doctor's words over and over. Aortic aneurysm. It sounded clinical, distant, but the fear it stirred in him was immediate and sharp.

Elena kept one hand on the wheel, the other resting gently on his knee. She didn't speak, didn't press. She knew he needed time to absorb it. But her eyes flicked toward him every few minutes, full of worry she couldn't hide. Jack wanted to say something, anything, but the words wouldn't come. All he could do was sit there, feeling the weight of uncertainty settle deeper into his chest. The road stretched ahead, cutting through the Dallas-Fort Worth metroplex. He just wanted to get home. Or better yet, wake up from this bad dream.

Elena felt helpless. She wished with every part of her being that she could make Jack better. But she also thought there must be a more logical reason. Something other than a stupid aortic aneurysm. The doctor had to be wrong. Jack had so many exams, tests, and blood work. *Why didn't any other doctor identify this possibility? Why did we move back here?* Elena wanted to blame everything and everyone. But the simple fact was, this was life. With general health, they had been fortunate. They had a healthy family, with only the kinds of injuries that could be explained and treated.

"I'm going to give Rachel a call," Elena blurted out. "She works at the Cleveland Clinic. She'll be able to give us some insight and maybe help us get some answers."

Jack sat in silence. He was tired. Physically and mentally. Tired of thinking about what-ifs and next steps.

"Do you want to stop for anything, babe?" she asked as he gazed out the window.

Jack briefly thought about it and replied, "I could use some Popeyes."

It was his go-to feel-good meal. Chicken strips, red beans and rice, a lovely buttery biscuit, and a lemonade. Some days, that was the best you could do.

21
BACK IN THE SADDLE

The walls of the house had started to close in. Jack had never been good at sitting still, and after months of recovery, rehab, and now restless pacing, the silence was beginning to wear him down. The pain in his abdomen was still there, sharp some days, dull and lingering on others, but it was the waiting that gnawed at him. Waiting for test results. Waiting for referrals. Waiting for answers that never seemed to come. He needed something to take his mind off it, something to remind him of who he was before the accident. Work seemed the logical answer.

He had been on medical leave since the day he was wheeled into the ER after the accident. His team had stepped up in his absence, and the university had been more than supportive. But now that full-time physical therapy was behind him, Jack felt the pull to return. Not full-time, not yet, but enough to feel useful again. Enough to feel like himself.

He picked up the phone and called Dr. Karen Leland, the university president. She answered on the second ring, her voice warm and familiar.

"Jack," she said, "it's good to hear from you. How are you holding up?"

"I'm getting there," he replied. "I wanted to talk to you about coming back. Just part-time for now. A few days a week. I think I'm ready."

There was a pause on the other end. Then, gently: "Are you sure? Your job isn't going anywhere, Jack. You can take all the time you need."

"I appreciate that," he said. "I really do. But I need this. I need something to focus on. I can still go to PT on Tuesdays and Thursdays.

I'll pace myself. I promise."

She sighed, but there was a smile in her voice. "Alright. Let's ease you back in. We'll keep it light. Just let me know if anything changes."

"Thank you," Jack said, and he meant it.

The next morning, he stood in front of the mirror, buttoning a shirt he hadn't worn in months. It felt strange and familiar at the same time, like trying on an old version of himself. His body was leaner now, more fragile in some ways, but his eyes were steady.

Elena walked into the bedroom and stared, then said, "You're looking good, Mr. Mercer. Are you ready?"

Jack smiled and paused. "I feel mentally ready. My body will catch up. A part of me just wants to get back into the swing of things. It took so long to get this job, plus it's darn near my dream job. I don't want to lose it."

"I think you're safe. Your team and everyone at the university loves you." Elena's words were confident, and they were what Jack needed.

He packed his bag, grabbed his ID badge, and kissed Elena goodbye. She didn't say much, just squeezed his hand and told him to call if he needed anything.

Walking into the office was surreal. The halls were quieter than he remembered, the fluorescent lights humming softly overhead. His team greeted him with cautious smiles and warm hugs, careful not to overwhelm him. They had questions, of course, but they didn't press. They were just glad to see him.

Jack settled into his desk, listened to the familiar whirring of his computer booting up. He took a deep breath. The pain in his abdomen was still there, a low throb beneath the surface, but he pushed it aside. He could manage it. He had to. He opened his inbox, scanned the backlog, and started replying, slowly, methodically. It wasn't much, but it was a start.

Then, as he typed, a familiar voice crept in—the quiet, cutting tone of his inner critic.

You're behind. You shouldn't have been out so long. You're not going to be able to keep up. You're slipping again.

Jack paused, fingers hovering over the keyboard. The thoughts came fast, sharp, and rehearsed. He knew them well. They'd been with him for years, always ready to twist progress into failure.

But this time, he caught them.

He leaned back in his chair, closed his eyes for a moment, and breathed through it. *Stay positive, Jack,* he told himself. *This is how it starts. One email. One step. You're here. You're trying.*

He opened his eyes and kept going. The critic would return—he knew that. But each time, he'd be ready.

He knew there would be days when the pain would flare up. Days when the fatigue would hit harder than expected. But he also knew he couldn't let fear dictate his life. Not anymore. He would take it day by day. Hour by hour if he had to. He had fought too hard.

It happened on a Wednesday, just after lunch. Jack had been reviewing a report when the pain hit, sharp and sudden, like a knife twisting deep in his abdomen. He tried to ignore it, to breathe through it like he always did, but this time it didn't fade. His vision blurred slightly, and a cold sweat broke out across his forehead.

Without a word, he stood and walked out of his office, down the hall, and into the stairwell. The door clicked shut behind him, sealing him in a space of concrete and silence. He sank onto the steps, his back against the wall, eyes closed. The pain made it hard to breathe, each inhale shallow and tight. *This is not it,* he whispered to himself, over and over, like a mantra.

The stairwell was cold, and the chill against his skin felt grounding, almost comforting. He sat there for nearly 20 minutes, focusing on his breathing, willing his body to calm down. Eventually, the pain dulled enough for him to stand. He moved slowly, gripping the railing for balance, and made his way back to his office. His receptionist looked up, concern etched across her face. "Are you okay, Jack? You look very pale." Jack forced a smile, his voice light. "I'm okay. Just a little tired. This work thing is exhausting," he said with a false laugh, then disappeared into his office before she could ask anything more.

Once the door to his office closed behind him, Jack sat down slowly, the false smile fading from his face. His hands trembled slightly as he reached for his phone. He didn't want to alarm Elena, but he needed to hear her voice—needed something steady to hold onto. He tapped her picture on his phone and waited, each ring seeming to stretch out longer than the last. When she answered, her voice was soft and familiar, like a warm blanket on a cold day. "Hey, you," she said.

Jack closed his eyes, letting the sound of her calm him. "Hey," he replied, his voice low. "I just ... I needed to hear your voice. It's been a rough day." He didn't go into detail, and she didn't press.

"I'm here," she said gently. "Always." For a moment, the pain didn't feel quite so heavy.

Elena shared how her day was going and what she had planned to make for dinner. Jack listened with his eyes closed. As if to a familiar, soothing song.

Jack said, "I'll see you soon. I'm heading home now."

"Be safe. Love you."

"Love you, too," he said, and ended the call.

Jack sent out one final email before he left. Gave some information to his receptionist to follow up on and then made his way to his truck.

He felt exhausted. It was a cooler day, and the breeze felt good. But Jack felt like he had just completed a marathon physical therapy session. His body ached, and he was still trying to control his breathing, taking deep breaths and slowly letting them out. When he got into his truck, he turned the A/C on high, pointed the air vents towards him, and pulled out of his parking space.

Jack couldn't remember feeling worse than he did that afternoon. He had made it through the rest of the day on autopilot, nodding through conversations, pretending everything was fine. But the truth was, he was barely holding it together. The pain in his abdomen had come roaring back—tight, hot, and radiating through his core like a live wire. Still, he told himself he could make it home. Just get to the truck. Just get home to Elena.

He didn't make it out of the parking garage.

The last thing he remembered was unlocking the door, sliding into the driver's seat, and gripping the steering wheel with both hands. The world tilted. His vision narrowed. Then, nothing.

The truck lurched forward, veering slightly before the front bumper clipped a concrete pillar and came to a stop with a dull, metallic thud. A security guard on patrol found him slumped over the wheel, unconscious, the engine still running. The ambulance arrived minutes later.

When Jack opened his eyes, the ceiling above him was white and unfamiliar. The beeping of monitors and the soft hiss of oxygen filled the room. Tubes ran from his arms, and a heart monitor blinked steadily beside him. Elena was sitting in the chair next to his bed, again, her hand wrapped tightly around his. Her eyes were red, but her grip was strong.

"You're awake," she whispered, brushing a hand through his hair.

Jack blinked slowly, trying to piece it all together. "What happened?"

"You passed out," she said gently. "In the garage. The truck hit a pillar. They brought you here."

He closed his eyes again, the weight of it all pressing down on him. He didn't need the doctors to tell him what was wrong. He already knew. So did Elena.

The doctors were running tests, bloodwork, imaging, cardiac monitoring. They spoke in cautious tones, using words like syncopal episode and vascular instability. But Jack could see it in their faces: they were worried. And so was he.

Because it was no longer a question of if, but when.

22
DENIED

Jack spent three days in the hospital under observation. The doctors ran every conceivable test—CT scans, ultrasounds, blood panels, cardiac monitoring. They poked and prodded, watched his vitals, and asked the same questions over and over. But no one could give him a definitive answer. The pain in his abdomen remained unpredictable and intense, and now there was a new concern: his blood pressure had spiked during the episode in the parking garage. The attending physician recommended starting him on blood pressure medication immediately.

Jack refused.

He wasn't being stubborn; he was being careful. "You don't even know what's causing this," he told them. "You're treating a symptom, not the problem." The doctors didn't argue, but they didn't agree, either. They discharged him with a stack of paperwork, a list of follow-up appointments, and a warning to "take it easy". Jack didn't need to be told. His body was already doing the talking.

When he got home, the house felt different. Quieter, darker. Elena helped him inside, made him tea, and insisted he rest. But Jack couldn't sit still. He wandered into the kitchen, where a small stack of unopened mail waited on the counter. One envelope stood out: it had the VA seal in one corner, and his name typed neatly across the front.

He opened it slowly, already bracing himself.

Specialist referral request denied.

The words hit like a punch to the gut. The specialist to whom the Dallas VA doctor had referred him, the one who might finally be able to confirm whether he had an aortic aneurysm, wasn't approved. The letter was cold, clinical, and final. No explanation. No alternative. Just a denial.

Jack stared at the page, jaw clenched, heart pounding. He felt the familiar surge of frustration rise in his chest. He had done everything right. He had followed the process, waited patiently, and tried to trust the system. And now, when he was closer than ever to getting real answers, the door had slammed shut.

Elena found him standing at the counter, the letter trembling in his hand. She didn't say anything at first, just took the paper, read it, and nodded once. Then she walked into the living room, grabbed her phone, and started dialing.

"Who are you calling?" Jack asked, his voice low.

"Rachel," she said. "Someone who actually gives a damn."

The call connected. "Hey, it's Elena. Yeah, it's been a while, I've been meaning to call you. Listen, I need your help. Jack's in trouble."

Her friend was a nurse at the Cleveland Clinic, someone she had served with during their time in Germany. They were nearly sisters, having been through numerous training exercises, medevac drills, and long nights in tents in the bitter cold of German winters. Elena trusted Rachel with her life, and now, she was going to trust her with Jack's.

Elena explained everything: the pain, the collapse, the hospital stay, the VA's denial, and what the Dallas VA doctor had mentioned. Her friend, Rachel, listened carefully, asked a few pointed questions, and then promised to reach out to a specialist she worked with. "We'll figure something out," she said. "You're not alone in this."

But Elena's voice grew more urgent, more personal. "Rachel, I'm scared. He's not saying it, but I can see it in his eyes. He's in pain every day, and no one's giving us answers. I need someone who will actually look at him like a human being, not a case file. I trust you. If there's anything, anything, you can do to help us get him seen, I'll owe you forever."

There was a pause on the other end, then Rachel's voice softened. "You don't owe me anything, El. You saved my ass more than once in Germany. I'll talk to Dr. Karim; he's one of the best doctors we've got. If

Jack's willing to come to Cleveland, I'll make sure he's seen. No red tape. No runaround. Just real answers."

Elena exhaled, her shoulders finally relaxing for the first time in days. "Thank you," she whispered. "You have no idea what this means to me."

"I do," Rachel replied. "And I've got you. I'm going to email you a medical release. I'll get his previous documentation and have Dr. Karim look it over. Just get him here."

Elena ended the call and turned to Jack, who had been listening quietly from the kitchen table. She didn't say anything right away, just walked over and wrapped her arms around him.

That evening, after dinner, Elena sat beside Jack on the couch, her legs tucked under her, a blanket draped across her lap. The television was on, but neither of them was really watching. She turned to him, her expression serious but hopeful.

"I talked to Rachel," she said softly. "She's willing to help. She's going to speak to a specialist at the Cleveland Clinic, a Dr. Karim. She says he would be willing to see you with no VA red tape. No waiting lists. He's a specialist in this area—if it's what we think it is."

Jack looked at her, his face unreadable. Claire jumped into his lamp and laid across his legs. He gently petted her head as she looked up at him.

"We'll figure out the billing and paperwork later," she added quickly. "I don't care what it costs. I just want you to be seen by someone who knows what they're doing."

Jack leaned back, staring at the ceiling for a long moment. "I appreciate it, El. I really do. But going all the way to Cleveland, on a hunch? Why not just go to one of the bigger hospitals in Dallas? They must have someone that knows what the hell they're talking about."

Elena paused, and took a slow deep breath. "It is a crazy thing to do, but I feel more secure with you in the hands of someone I know and trust. I'm tired of playing the guessing game with the VA and whatever referral they approve or don't approve."

Jack looked in her eyes, he saw her focus and determination. He knew she wasn't going to let it go. "I need to think about it overnight," he said finally. His voice was quiet but steady. "I'm up for a gamble, but can I make it there? That's the part I'm not sure about."

He rubbed his abdomen gently, the pain still lingering like a shadow. "Flying doesn't feel like the right move, too much pressure, too many variables. But driving ... maybe. If we take it slow."

Elena nodded, not pushing. "Okay. We'll take it one step at a time."

Restless, Jack lay awake that night, gazing at the ceiling fan drifting in slow motion above him. He thought about the hospital, the stairwell, the truck, the letter. He thought about Elena, how she never gave up, how she kept fighting even when he couldn't. And he thought about the trip ahead. It was long. Uncertain. But maybe it was the way forward.

The next morning, the smell of coffee pulled him from sleep. He shuffled into the kitchen, still stiff, still sore. Elena was standing at the stove in a worn Army T-shirt, her hair pulled back, humming softly.

Jack poured a cup of coffee, took a sip, and leaned against the counter. He watched her for a moment, then asked, "When do we leave?"

She turned, eyes wide, and smiled. Relieved, proud, and a little scared, too. "We'll pack today," she said. "We can be on the road early tomorrow morning."

Jack nodded. "Sounds like a plan."

23
HEADING NORTH

They left Fort Worth at four in the morning, the city still cloaked in darkness, the streets quiet save for the occasional delivery truck or early commuter. Jack sat in the passenger seat, bundled in a hoodie, a travel pillow tucked behind his neck. Elena drove, her hands steady on the wheel, her eyes focused on the road ahead. The GPS glowed softly on the dashboard, already charting the long stretch of highway that would carry them across five states and a little over 1,200 miles.

Elena had packed snacks, reading material, and had the passenger seat set up like a personal spa retreat for Jack. Driving long distances wasn't her favorite. This was different, though, and the thought of the distance never crossed her mind.

They merged onto I-30 heading east, the skyline of Dallas fading behind them. Jack sipped from a thermos of coffee, the warmth helping to settle his nerves. His abdomen still ached—a dull, persistent throb that reminded him with every bump and turn that time was not on his side. But he was doing this. They were doing this.

By the time they crossed into Arkansas, the sun was up, casting golden light across the flat fields and pine forests. They passed through Texarkana, then Little Rock, where they picked up Interstate 40 and continued east. The miles rolled by in a blur of highway signs, gas station stops, and quiet conversation. Jack dozed off and on, waking each time with a wince, shifting in his seat to find a position that didn't hurt. Elena kept driving, her focus unwavering, checking on him every so often with a glance or a gentle touch on his arm.

In Memphis, they stopped for a quick lunch of sandwiches and water. Jack wished he was in the mood for BBQ, but the pain had dulled his appetite. He forced down a few bites of sandwich, for Elena's sake. She didn't push him. She just sat beside him in the booth, her hand resting on his knee, her presence a constant reassurance.

By late afternoon, they reached Nashville, the traffic thickening as they navigated the city's winding interchanges. From there, they picked up I-65 north toward Bowling Green, Kentucky. The sun had dipped low in the sky, casting long shadows across the road. Jack was exhausted, his body aching from the hours in the car, but he was determined to make it to Bowling Green. That was the plan.

They pulled into his best friend's driveway just after 8:30 p.m. The porch light was on, and the front door opened before they even got out of the car. One of the legendary *Horsemen*, Graham, stood there with his arms crossed and a wide grin on his face. "Took you long enough," he said, pulling Jack into a careful hug. Jack winced but smiled. It felt good to see a familiar face.

They spent the evening catching up, sitting on the back porch with blankets and mugs of tea. Jack didn't say much; he was too tired. But he listened, and that was enough. Elena filled Graham in on the plan: they'd leave early in the morning and drive straight through to Cleveland. Her friend Rachel had told her to bring Jack straight to the emergency room when they arrived. "They'll be expecting him," she said.

Jack was too worn down to fight the plan, and deep inside he knew it was the right move. He just hoped his body would hold out long enough to get there.

The next morning, Graham had the coffee made and supplied them with more snacks and a couple of sandwiches. Jack and Graham hugged for a long time. "I love you, brother," Graham said.

"Love you, too," Jack replied. Then he carefully walked down the steps towards the car.

Again they were on the road before sunrise. I-65 took them north through Louisville, the Ohio River glinting in the early light. From there, they merged onto I-71, the final stretch that would carry them all the way to Cleveland.

Elena called their oldest daughter, Lily. "We're headed to Cleveland, sweetie," she said. "Dad's going to be seen at the Cleveland Clinic." They spoke for a little while and then the call ended. "Let's plan a night to have dinner with Lily," Elena said to Jack.

"Sounds good." Jack was half asleep and ready for the drive to be over.

The landscape changed as they drove, full now of rolling hills, dense woods, and small towns tucked between exits. Jack watched it all pass by in silence, his emotions drifting between hope and fear.

By the time they reached the outskirts of Cleveland, the sky had turned grey, and a light drizzle was misting the windshield. I-71 blended into I-90 and then off onto Highway 20. Elena read each street sign as she listened to the GPS. A right on East 89th street and another on Cedar Avenue. Elena's phone buzzed. Rachel. "We're here," Elena said. "Pulling into the ER now."

Rachel met them at the entrance, her nurse's badge clipped to her scrubs, her face a mix of concern and determination. "Let's get him inside," she said, opening the passenger door. Jack nearly fell out of the car; he was pale and out of it. Another nurse ran to help Rachel get him in a wheelchair.

Elena had been so focused on getting to the hospital that she hadn't noticed Jack slowly slumping down, his skin growing pale and clammy.

A young doctor met them outside the ER, immediately checking Jack's pulse, temperature, and abdomen. "We've got a rupture," he yelled in a commanding voice. "Prep OR 3." Quickly, a team of nurses and doctors transferred him to a gurney, ripped open his shirt, and began to prep him for surgery.

"Wait. Wait, what?" Elena's words fell unheard amid the commotion.

A nurse stopped her at a set of double doors. "We'll take it from here," she said.

Elena froze in place. Helpless. Mad at herself. "Why the hell didn't I drive faster?" she wailed. As they rushed her husband down the corridor, Elena suddenly snapped out of it.

"Jack, you have angels! Remember, you have angels, Jack!"

Her words echoed down the hall. From behind, a hand reached out and gently grabbed her shoulder. She spun to see Graham.

"You didn't think I was going to let you have all this excitement to yourself, did you?"

Graham had left after them. Called in to work, explained what was going on, and headed out. He and Jack had been through more hell than anyone could imagine. There was no way his brother and Elena were going through this alone.

"Oh, my God! Thank you! Thank you!" Elena said as she burst into tears. All the emotion she had been trying to control came pouring forth. She was mad, scared, and exhausted. Why didn't she notice Jack had gotten worse? She cursed herself in her mind and prayed she had made it here in time.

"He'll be okay," Graham said. "I know my boy, and this isn't the end." Graham's words were comforting, and Elena knew he was right. Jack had been through so much. She thought about his last suicide attempt. The darkness that had enshrouded him and his battle to overcome his demons.

This can't be it. He's too tough. There's more we need to do.

24
THE BREAKING POINT

Elena stood in the sterile hospital hallway, her arms wrapped tightly around herself, as if by doing so she could somehow hold her own heart together. But her mind wasn't in the present; it had drifted, unbidden, back to that morning. That awful, quiet morning when everything changed.

October 21, 2016

She had known something was wrong the moment Jack stepped out of the bedroom. He moved like a man underwater—slow, heavy, distant. His eyes, usually sharp and alert, were dull and unfocused, like he was looking through her, not at her. He barely touched his coffee and didn't respond when she asked if he wanted breakfast.

The silence between them was thick, unnatural. As they drove to the bus stop, the tension in the car was suffocating. Jack stared out the window, jaw clenched, hands resting motionless in his lap. Elena's fingers gripped the steering wheel tighter with every passing block.

She couldn't take it anymore. "Please," she said, her voice cracking, "please tell me what's wrong."

Jack didn't answer. He just kept staring ahead.

She tried again, more desperate this time. "Jack, talk to me," she pleaded. "You're scaring me." That's when it happened. Without warning, he slammed his fist into the dashboard, once, twice, again and again, until the plastic cracked and his knuckles split.

Elena screamed, pulling the car over, her heart racing. Jack was crying now, his face twisted in anguish, his voice raw and broken. "I'm done," he shouted. "I'm tired. I can't do this anymore."

The words echoed in the car like a gunshot. Elena froze, her mind racing, unsure of what to do. She reached for him, but he pulled away, curling into himself like a wounded animal. She had never seen him like this. Not even after the deployments. This was something deeper. Something darker.

She pulled out her phone with shaking hands and searched for veteran crisis help, anything, anyone. She found a number and called. A calm voice answered, and Elena explained everything in a rush of panic and tears. The woman on the other end was kind but firm.

"Take him to the nearest emergency room," she said. "Don't let him out of your sight. Don't let him leave." Elena hung up and turned the car around, driving as fast as she could toward Marin General.

Jack didn't speak. He mumbled to himself, fragments of sentences that made no sense, names she didn't recognize, places he hadn't been in years. He was somewhere else entirely, lost in a memory or a nightmare she couldn't reach. When they arrived at the ER, she ran inside, shouting for help. Nurses rushed out with a wheelchair, and Jack didn't resist. He just sat there, eyes vacant, lips moving in a whisper only he could hear. The doctors took him in immediately. Elena followed, answering questions, signing forms, trying to stay strong. But inside, she was unraveling.

They admitted him to the mental health unit that night. She wasn't allowed to stay. She kissed his forehead, whispered that she loved him, and watched as the doors closed behind him. Then, she went into the parking lot and cried until her body ached.

The first few days were a blur for Elena—filled with phone calls, paperwork, and long, anxious hours waiting for updates. The attending psychiatrist kept her informed, but she wasn't allowed to see Jack. His condition was too fragile, and the hospital's policy required a brief stabilization period before visitors were permitted.

The doctors said he was experiencing a severe depressive episode, likely triggered by a combination of chronic pain, PTSD, and emotional exhaustion. Elena didn't need the diagnosis. She already knew: Jack had reached his boiling point. The weight of everything—his injuries, the pain, the uncertainty, the years of holding it all in—had finally crushed him. His demons had clawed their way to the surface, and he had nothing left to fight them with.

During those first three days, Jack was quiet, withdrawn, sometimes angry, sometimes impassive. He barely spoke and refused to eat. The medications hadn't taken hold, and he seemed lost in a fog of despair. Elena felt helpless, clinging to the doctor's reassurances that this was not uncommon in the early stages of treatment.

Then, on the fourth day, Elena was finally allowed to visit. She walked into the unit with her heart pounding, unsure of what she would find. But something had shifted. Jack had eaten some yogurt for breakfast. He had responded to a nurse with a faint smile. The clouds had begun to break.

When Elena saw him, her eyes welled with tears. Jack looked pale and tired, but he was present—really there. Without saying a word, she rushed to him and wrapped her arms around him in a long, trembling hug. For the first time in days, she felt the weight in her chest begin to lift.

During visits she sat by his bed, read to him, brought him photos, reminded him of who he was. Slowly, painfully, he began to come back. Not all at once. Not completely. But enough. Enough to look her in the eyes again. Enough to say her name. Enough to whisper, "I'm sorry."

Elena never blamed him. Not for a second. She knew what war did to people. But knowing didn't make it easier. Loving someone through that kind of darkness was its own kind of battle. And she had fought it with everything she had.

Jack's first real meal was a toasted peanut butter and jelly sandwich, a side of blueberries, and cottage cheese. For the next week he ate the exact same meal. It was comfort food, something he had quite often when he had lived with Grandma Treva. He told Elena about how he and grandma had sat outside, talking about life and the garden, while eating.

Elena told their girls about the situation. Not in detail, but enough so they understood. She also called his best friend, Graham, and let him know. A couple of times a week, Jack's sister and brother-in-law would visit, and Elena came every visitation time.

"How are you doing, babe?" Elena would ask him each visit.

"I'm learning how to get better," he replied every time, with a real smile, and with real warmth in his eyes.

In many ways it was the longest two weeks of Elena's life. It seemed at once to go on and on, an endless expanse of anxiety and worry, and also to somehow fly by in a confusion of overwhelming emotions and warped time.

The day before Jack was discharged, Elena sat across from Dr. Patel, Jack's psychiatrist in the mental health unit, in a small consultation room. Jack was beside her, quiet but attentive, his hands folded in his lap. The doctor had a calm, reassuring presence and spoke with the kind of clarity Elena appreciated.

"We're seeing good signs," Dr. Patel began. "Jack's responding to the medication, and he's been engaging in group therapy. That's why we feel confident about moving him to outpatient care. But I want to be clear—this next phase is just as important."

Elena nodded, leaning forward. "What should we expect? What can I do to help him at home?"

Dr. Patel smiled gently. "Structure is key. Jack will have weekly therapy sessions, and we've enrolled him in a cognitive behavioral skills group. He'll need time to adjust, and there may be setbacks. That's normal. What matters most is consistency—and compassion."

Jack glanced at Elena, then back at the doctor. "Will I ever feel normal again?" he asked quietly.

"You're already on your way," Dr. Patel said. "Recovery isn't about going back to who you were—it's about building something new, with tools you didn't have before."

Elena reached for Jack's hand. "We'll figure it out together."

Dr. Patel handed Elena a folder filled with resources—emergency contacts, medication schedules, signs to watch for, and tips for caregivers. "You're not alone in this," he said. "And neither is Jack."

But despite Elena's preparation, nothing could fully ease the uncertainty of those first few days home. Jack was quieter, more introspective. He followed his treatment plan diligently—attending therapy sessions, journaling, and practicing mindfulness exercises—but Elena understood his healing wouldn't be linear. He had to learn new ways of thinking, rebuild his confidence, and eventually, forgive himself.

She stood by him through it all, not just as a caregiver, but as someone who believed in his ability to find peace again. Their life had changed, but they were facing it together—one day at a time.

She witnessed his progress, and at times his regression. "I'm sorry you got stuck with me," he said on one of their nightly walks. "I want to be better and be the man you deserve."

"You are. And even more," she peacefully replied, caressing his arm.

Now, standing in the hallway of a hospital in Ohio, waiting for word from the doctors on the state of the aortic rupture, fear crept in. Jack could simply slip away, the promise of peaceful eternal sleep too compelling against a lifetime of pain.

But Elena remembered how strong Jack was. She remembered that no matter what he faced, he fought. He fought for himself, and he fought to come back to her. Jack loved her so deeply that, each time, he transcended the pain like a resurrecting phoenix flying toward the sun of her arms.

Jack liked to think he wasn't good enough for Elena, but Elena knew—he would be her hero until her dying day.

25
THE EDGE OF EVERYTHING

For Jack, the pain had come like a lightning strike—sudden, searing, and absolute. He wasn't even able to speak. It was as if one moment he had been listening to Elena chatting as she drove, and the next he was clutching his abdomen, gasping for air. His body seized, and he collapsed against the seat, eyes wide with panic. He could vaguely see Elena talking on the phone, and then there was silence.

Around them the staff erupted into action. Elena's voice couldn't cut through the chaos; she was terrified, and Jack couldn't respond. The pain was too much. It felt like something inside him had torn open.

And it had.

The aneurysm had ruptured.

Within minutes, Jack was on a gurney, hurtling through the corridors of the Cleveland Clinic. The trauma team surrounded him, ripping open his shirt, inserting IV lines, pushing fluids, calling out vitals. His blood pressure was plummeting. His skin had gone clammy and pale. He was losing blood fast, internally, and they all knew it. "We've got a rupture, prep OR 3 now!" shouted the doctor.

Jack could vaguely hear muffled chatter. With barely open eyes, he saw blurred figures around him. But there was one over him that was brighter than the others. He heard a gentle whisper, faint, distant, but he could make it out: "You'll be okay, sweetie."

Elena ran alongside the gurney until they reached the surgical wing, where a nurse gently stopped her at the double doors. "We'll take it from here," she said. Elena nodded, frozen in place, watching as Jack disappeared. Rachel appeared moments later, her face grim. "They'll do everything they can," she said. "He's in the best hands."

In Jack's vision, a soft-lit figure followed him into the operating room. "You're okay, sweetie," it said again. He tried to reach out, but his arms wouldn't move. Then, the figure faded away as Jack went under.

In the operating room, the team moved with practiced urgency under overhead lights that bathed the sterile field in bright white. Dr. Karim entered briskly, already sliding on gloves and a gown. His voice was calm but firm.

"Vitals?" he asked, as he stepped up to the table.

"BP 70 over 40 and falling. Heart rate 130. He's bleeding into the retroperitoneal space," the circulating nurse replied.

"Let's move. Midline laparotomy. Get me vascular clamps, suction, and a Dacron graft kit. Notify the blood bank—we'll need at least six units of O-negative on standby."

The anesthesiologist, Dr. Lin, worked quickly to stabilize Jack's airway. She inserted an endotracheal tube, confirming placement with capnography and auscultation. She adjusted the ventilator settings, tidal volume, respiratory rate, and FiO2 while simultaneously titrating vasopressors to support Jack's plummeting blood pressure.

The surgical techs laid out instruments with precision: scalpels, retractors, Metzenbaum scissors, DeBakey forceps, vascular clamps, and needle drivers. The room buzzed with controlled intensity.

Dr. Karim made the first incision, a vertical midline laparotomy, running from the bottom of the breastbone to just above the pubic bone. He cut through the skin, subcutaneous fat, and fascia, then used electrocautery to control bleeding from small vessels. As he entered the peritoneal cavity, a rush of dark, free blood spilled out.

"Massive hemoperitoneum," he muttered, indicating significant internal bleeding. "Suction."

The suction cannula slurped loudly as the surgical assistant cleared the field. Dr. Karim retracted the bowel loops to the left, exposing the retroperitoneum, the back of the abdominal cavity. The source of the bleeding was now clear: a ruptured abdominal aortic aneurysm, just below the renal arteries.

"Clamp above the renal arteries. We need proximal control," Dr. Karim ordered. "Expose the suprarenal aorta."

The assistant carefully dissected the tissue around the aorta, avoiding the inferior vena cava and renal veins. A Satinsky clamp was placed just above the renal arteries to control proximal flow. Another clamp was applied distally, just above the aortic bifurcation.

"Time of cross-clamp: 14:42," the nurse called out.

The room was hot and tense, filled with the rhythmic beeping of monitors and the soft hiss of the ventilator. Jack's blood pressure hovered dangerously low despite aggressive fluid resuscitation and vasopressors. Every second was dangerous.

"Rupture's about six centimeters. Wall's completely compromised," Dr. Karim said, inspecting the aneurysm. "We're going to resect the aneurysm and replace it with a Dacron graft."

The aneurysm sac was opened, revealing a large volume of thrombus. Dr. Karim evacuated the thrombus and debrided the friable aortic wall. The renal arteries were carefully preserved.

"Get me the 20mm Dacron tube graft. Trim it to length."

The synthetic graft was soaked in saline and trimmed to match the resected segment. Karim began suturing the proximal end to the healthy aorta using 4-0 polypropylene suture in a continuous, hemostatic fashion. Each stitch had to be precise. Too loose and it would leak, too tight and it could tear the fragile tissue.

"Proximal anastomosis is secure. Let's move to the distal end."

The distal end of the graft was sewn to the aorta just above the iliac bifurcation. The clamps were slowly released, first proximally, then distally. Blood surged through the graft.

"Check for bleeding," Dr. Karim said.

The assistant irrigated the field with warm saline. "The field's dry. Graft's holding."

The room let out a silent breath.

"Good. Let's close."

The team began the long process of closing the incision. Dr. Karim closed the posterior peritoneum, then the fascia with heavy interrupted sutures. The subcutaneous tissue was irrigated and closed in layers.

Finally, the skin was approximated with staples.

"BP's up to 95 over 60. Heart rate's coming down," Dr. Lin reported. "He's stabilizing."

Dr. Karim exhaled slowly. "Let's get him to the ICU. Keep him intubated. Start him on broad-spectrum antibiotics and monitor for reperfusion injury. Watch the renal function; he was clamped above it for over 30 minutes."

The team wheeled Jack out of the OR, monitors beeping, IV lines running, ventilator hissing. The rupture had been repaired. The graft was secure. But the next 24 hours would be critical.

Four hours, 55 minutes, and 36 seconds after the first incision, the red light above the OR door finally went dark. Elena stood as Dr. Karim stepped into the hallway, removing his surgical cap. His face was lined with fatigue, but his eyes were steady.

"He made it," he said. "It was a significant rupture, but we were able to repair it with a synthetic graft. He lost a lot of blood, but he's stable now. He's going to need time to recover, but he's alive."

Elena's knees buckled, and Graham caught her, guiding her to a chair. Tears streamed down her face. Jack was alive.

Jack awakened to the soft beeping of monitors and the familiar sterile scent of a hospital room. His throat was dry, his body heavy, but he was alive. Tubes ran from his arms, and a thick bandage stretched across his abdomen. He turned his head slowly and saw Elena sitting beside him, her hand wrapped around his. Standing next to her was Graham.

"You're okay," she whispered, brushing a tear from her cheek. "You're okay."

Jack tried to speak, but only a rasp came out. Elena leaned in, her forehead resting against his.

"You scared the hell out of me," she said, her voice trembling.

"Let's not do this anymore," added Graham.

Jack closed his eyes. He didn't remember much, just the flash of pain, the panic, the cold rush of knowing it might be the end. He tried again to speak.

"Relax, my brother. Your voice will come," Graham said as he gently patted his leg.

"Rest, babe. Just rest for now." Elena kissed Jack's forehead again and whispered, "I love you."

Jack blinked, and he could hear himself saying, "I love you," but no words were coming out.

He closed his eyes again and slept.

As Jack drifted in and out of sedation in the ICU, his mind carried him somewhere far from the antiseptic white walls and the quiet hum of machines. He was a boy again, no more than 10, standing tall in his dust-covered boots at the rodeo grounds in Wellington, Texas. The late summer sun hung low in the sky, casting long shadows across the arena. He could hear the creak of saddle leather, the distant clang of gates, and the low murmur of voices, ranchers, cowboys, and kids just like him, all drawn to the magic of the rodeo. The air smelled like dirt, sweat, and livestock. He remembered the way the dirt felt under his feet, how warm and soft it was as it ran through his hands, and how his heart raced every time a bronc burst from the chute, hooves kicking, riders holding on for dear life.

He was sitting on the top rail of the fence, legs swinging, a Dr. Pepper in one hand and a bag of jerky in the other. His uncle stood beside him, pointing out riders he knew, telling stories about the old days. Jack had wanted to be one of them—fearless, wild, free.

He remembered the way the crowd roared when a rider made the full eight seconds, the way the dust rose in golden clouds behind the broncs. It was a place where time slowed down, where the world felt simple and wide open. In that dream, there was no pain. There were no hospitals, no war. Just the sound of boots climbing fences, the smell of horses, and the feeling that anything was possible.

26
GOING HOME

Jack's recovery from the rupture was slow and cautiously monitored. The surgery had saved his life, but it had also taken a toll on him physically. Jack didn't have many tolls left to give.

The first few days in the ICU were a blur of pain management, vital checks, and whispered conversations between nurses and doctors. Tubes ran from his arms, monitors beeped steadily beside him, and every breath felt like it had to be earned. As a kid he'd listened to stories from old cowboys about being kicked in the head and chest by crazy broncs. He wondered if this was what it felt like. Maybe life was giving him what he aimed for, one way or the other.

Dr. Karim stopped by daily, checking the incision site, reviewing scans, and adjusting medications. "You were lucky," he said more than once. "If you'd gotten here even an hour later ..." He didn't finish the sentence. He didn't have to. Jack understood how close he'd come.

Graham stayed for a couple days, hanging out and talking to Jack, keeping him company while Elena got a break. His oldest daughter, Lily, came by multiple times.

Elena spent almost every minute by his side. She slept in a chair, brought him ice chips, helped him sit up when the pain was too much to do it alone.

"You can't make these hospital visits a regular thing, babe. These chairs are ruining my sleep," she said, laughing lightly, as she brushed his cheek. Her eyes were full of light and love.

Jack looked at her and smiled, though his words were raspy and quiet. "I heard your voice." He paused to wet his lips. "I heard you yell out about the angels."

Elena held back tears and gave Jack a kiss on his forehead. "I wanted to remind you that you're not alone."

Rachel checked in constantly, making sure Jack had the best care, advocating for him. She was able to get him enrolled in a study on aortic aneurysms, which saved Jack and Elena a lot of time and money. The nurses came to know Elena by name. She was the one who asked the hard questions, who kept the charts straight, who made sure Jack never felt alone.

Elena wanted to understand why this happened. Why wasn't it detected by all the other doctors? And most importantly, could it happen again?

"Jack's aortic aneurysm was unique in the sense it did not bulge or swell up like most," Dr. Karim said. "So detecting it would have been difficult, unless one was specifically looking for it. In Jack's case there are a couple possibilities as to why. He's not a smoker and doesn't have a history of smoking, so I am ruling those out."

Dr. Karim asked about Jack's military service and if he might have been exposed to bad air or chemicals, which would have made breathing hard.

"I was deployed multiple times. The first was Desert Storm in the early '90s. We were always around burning oil wells in Kuwait, and we maneuvered in areas where chemical agents had been used during the Iraq and Iranian war." Jack's voice was still a bit raspy, but it came through with a ringing, startling clarity to Dr. Karim.

For a brief moment, Dr. Omar Hassan Al-Karim thought of his dad, and imagined once again the challenges his father had likely gone through. "I'm sorry to hear that," he said. "My father served in the Iraqi Army. He was forced to serve." The words just came out. Dr. Karim wasn't even sure why he had mentioned this.

Jack could see the sadness in his eyes. "Wars are fought by people who have nothing to do with the issues. We're tools for our governments. Innocent people pay the price, while the leaders sit safely far away."

Dr. Karim nodded. "I agree."

Both men seemed lost in their thoughts. After a moment, Elena spoke up. "Okay, so there are a few possibilities as to why this happened to Jack, but can it happen again?"

"My apologies, Elena." Dr. Karim's voice was back to being focused. "It can. However, with maintaining a healthy lifestyle the risks can be dramatically reduced."

He went on to explain that aortic aneurysms can be associated with other vascular issues, such as popliteal artery aneurysms. With age came a higher risk, and now that this event was in his records, Jack's other doctors would know what to monitor.

Jack and Elena thanked Dr. Karim for everything and then the unexpectedly wistful doctor headed outside for some fresh air. It was a cold morning, a frosty chill coming in off the lake. He thought about the few memories he had of his dad. The stories his mom had shared. He wished his family could have left Iraq sooner, much sooner. *But I'm better, Baba, every day.*

Jack spent nearly two weeks at the Cleveland Clinic. After the first critical days came a slow climb back: sitting up, standing, walking a few steps with help. Yet again, each milestone felt like a victory. The pain was sharp, but different now. It was no longer the unpredictable agony of an aneurysm, but a clean, healing kind of pain that came with stitches and scar tissue.

By the end of the second week, Dr. Karim cleared him for discharge. "You're stable," he said. "But you're not out of the woods. You'll need follow-up care. I'll be sending your information to your doctor; you will need to participate in cardiac rehab, and it's going to take time. You strike me as a man with little patience for things like this."

Elena laughed as Dr. Karim continued. "Take baby steps. If something does not feel right, if there's any unexplained pain, go to the ER."

Jack nodded. He understood. He felt like each ER visit changed him. He was becoming a bit more aware, patient, and comprehending of how precious and fragile life was. But he was still alive and kicking. That meant something.

The morning they left Cleveland, the sky was overcast and cool.

Elena packed the car carefully, making sure Jack had pillows, water, and his medications within reach. Rachel hugged them both tightly in the parking garage. "You've got a long road ahead," she said, "but you're not walking it alone. Call me if you have any questions or concerns."

They jumped on I-71 south, retracing the route they had driven just weeks earlier, but everything felt different now. The tension that had hung over them like a storm cloud was gone, replaced by a quiet, cautious relaxation. Jack slept through much of the first leg, the hum of the road lulling him into a light, dreamless rest. Elena drove with one hand on the wheel and the other occasionally reaching over to check on him.

They stopped overnight in Bowling Green again, staying with Graham once more, who greeted them with a delicate hug and a hot meal. Jack moved slowly, carefully, but he was upright, walking on his own, and that alone felt like a miracle.

The next day, before driving out, Graham gave them a cooler full of home-cooked food. "Just some snacks to help get you home," he said.

Elena and Jack continued the journey, through Nashville, Little Rock, and finally back into Texas. The landscape grew more familiar with every mile: wide skies, land slowly flattening, an occasional windmill spinning lazily in the distance. When they finally pulled into their driveway in Fort Worth, the sun was setting, casting a warm orange glow across the front porch.

Jack sat in the passenger seat for a moment, staring at the house. It looked the same, but he felt different. It was home, but it wasn't. The front porch still had the wind chimes Elena had hung, and the rosemary bush by the steps had grown wild in their absence. The curtains in the living room were drawn just the way he liked them, and the welcome mat hadn't moved an inch. But something inside him had shifted. The house felt like a stranger, like a place he had heard about but never quite become familiar with.

Elena came around to his side, opened the door, and offered her hand. "Ready?" she asked.

Jack took her hand, slowly stepping out of the car. His body ached, his strength was still returning, but he stood tall.

"Yeah," he said. "I'm ready."

He moved slowly into the house, while Elena grabbed the bags. When she was inside, she opened up some windows and the back door for fresh air. The breeze drifted in, carrying the scent of warm pine and distant chimney smoke. Light spilled across the hardwood floors, warm and semi-familiar.

Jack wandered into the living room, his eyes scanning the space. The couch was still angled toward the television, the bookshelf still crowded with novels and old photo albums. But something felt off. It was like stepping into a memory—one he wasn't sure he belonged to anymore. The house hadn't changed, but he had. The silence within the walls felt unwelcoming, and the comfort of coming home was replaced with a quiet uncertainty.

He sat down slowly, letting his fingers trace the armrest of the couch he used to sink into after long days. It was good to be back, but it didn't feel like home. He knew it would take time to reconnect with this space, to have it feel like his and Elena's place again.

"Are you hungry, babe?" she asked, as Jack settled into his spot on the couch.

"I'm good. Just tired."

He texted the friends who were watching their dog, Claire, letting them know they were home and asking if they could bring her home tomorrow morning. That would help.

Elena finally settled down on the couch next to Jack. She gently leaned on his shoulder.

"Are you happy here?" Jack asked Elena. She lifted her head and looked at him.

"As long as we're together."

Jack stopped her mid-sentence. "I mean, are you happy living here? In Fort Worth."

"You know how I feel about Texas. Why do you ask?"

Jack paused for a few seconds, trying to form the right words. He didn't want to stress Elena out. She had enough on her plate.

"I've been in a major car accident. Had this damn rupture. With each incident I think about the what-ifs. I think about how life is so short and how we deserve to be in our happy place."

Elena looked at Jack with inquisitive eyes. "What are you getting at, Jack?"

"Leaving California sucked. Whether it was right or wrong to move is neither here nor there. It doesn't matter. What I'm trying to say is we deserve to be where we are happy." Jack took a deep breath, his voice breaking. "Let's find a place in California where we can live. It's where we want to be. We've made things happen before. And we can make this happen, too."

They stared at one another, each with questions and comments in their eyes. "I know it'll be a challenge to find work. Honestly, I don't like giving up this job that I love. But I also know where we've been the happiest."

Elena didn't answer at first. She rested her head on Jack's shoulder. She repeated his words in her head.

"Let's sleep on this, Jack. We've had a long trip, and we need it."

Jack woke early the following morning. He slowly rolled out of bed, not only due to his physical condition but also because he did not want to wake Elena. He heard the truck pull up at 7 a.m. Claire's entire body wagged as she ran to the front door. "Hey there, how you doing, girl?" Jack asked, gently bending his head to look in her eyes. "Sorry if you were worried. I'm happy to be back, too."

He brought Claire into the kitchen and started some coffee. He petted Claire while he waited, relaxing into it, and his mind clicked into place. Opening his computer, he began searching and estimating the cost of living around Sacramento, California. He knew it was more affordable than living in Marin County, and it was close to his sister and only a couple hours each way to the ocean and the mountains.

With the sale of their home, along with his retirement and disability income, they could find a little place. His only question was whether Elena would be on board. Would she think it was just one of his spur-of-the-moment notions? But Jack knew she loved California. In his mind, the risk was worth the reward.

Elena reached over to check on Jack and was briefly caught off guard that he wasn't in bed beside her. She walked out to the living room and saw him at the kitchen table. He looked focused.

A grin appeared on her face. "You found a place in California already." It wasn't even a question.

Jack gave a slight laugh. "I think I have."

Over breakfast they discussed options and possible scenarios. Each of them knew the risk. And each one knew the reward.

"I know it's cheesy to say," Jack said, "but life is too short. If I've learned anything over these past couple of years, it's that."

Elena looked at her plate and nodded. "I agree," she said. "Let's call your sister and get her two cents."

Jack agreed. They finished their breakfast, making small talk about what they needed from the grocery store and their plans for the week. Then Jack grabbed his phone, pulled up his sister's number, and gave her a call. She answered on the second ring.

"Hey you, what are you up to? How are you feeling?" Elizabeth was happy to hear her little brother's voice. "I was thinking about you two this morning."

"Elena and I want to run something by you. Get your input."

"Yes! You can stay with us as long as you need. We have the room."

Elizabeth's words startled him. "How do you even know what I'm going to say?"

"I can just tell. And when I was thinking about you two, I wished you hadn't moved. I understand why you needed to, but still. You two belong out here." Her words were definitive.

Elena replied, "We have some things to figure out. The wild card is selling the house, however fast or slow that happens."

They talked for an hour. Making plans for all kinds of what-ifs. Talking through scenarios. Throughout the call Elena and Jack looked at one another and smiled. Smiles full of love. Smiles that said, *"We got this."*

27
THE RETURN

The air in Baghdad was thick with dust and ringing with city noise. Dr. Omar Hassan Al-Karim stepped off the plane and into the world that had shaped him, now unfamiliar in its rhythm. But Iraq had not changed as much as he had. Cleveland had become his home, with its cold winters, its quiet suburbs, and its hospitals where he had built a life of purpose and healing. But here, in the land of his birth, he felt like a visitor in a dream he could barely remember.

He spent the night in a modest hotel near the airport, unable to sleep. The city hummed with life outside his window—cars honking, vendors shouting. It was familiar, yet distant, like a song he once knew by heart but could no longer remember. Restless, he ventured out to a night market that pulsed with color and sound. Strings of lights hung overhead, casting a warm glow over rows of stalls packed with spices, sweets, and handwoven goods. The air was thick with the scent of grilled lamb, cardamom, and rosewater. Children out late darted between vendors, laughter echoing through the narrow alleys, while old men sipped tea and played backgammon on worn wooden tables.

Omar wandered slowly, taking it all in. He paused at a stall selling scarves—bright, intricate patterns woven into soft fabric. One caught his eye: deep blue with gold threading, delicate and bold. He thought of his mother, how she used to wrap scarves around her shoulders even in the summer, saying they made her feel elegant.

"How much for this one?" he asked the vendor, a wiry man with a salt-and-pepper beard and a mischievous smile.

"Ah, for you, my friend, only 25,000 dinars," the man said, clearly expecting a counteroffer.

Omar raised an eyebrow. "25? That's a bit steep, don't you think?"

The vendor laughed. "It's the finest quality. Look at the stitching!"

Omar ran his fingers over the fabric, then smiled. "I'll give you 15."

The man clutched his chest in mock offense. "Fifteen? You wound me!"

They went back and forth, the haggling playful, almost musical. In the end, Omar paid 18,000 and walked away with the scarf folded neatly in a paper bag.

As he made his way back to the hotel, the city still buzzing around him, Omar felt something stir inside—a flicker of connection, of belonging. Baghdad had changed, but the people felt familiar.

The next morning, he rented a dusty white sedan and began the long drive east to Balad Ruz, the village where he was born. The road stretched out like a ribbon of memory, winding through the arid plains and low hills of Diyala Province. Along the way, he passed olive groves, crumbling checkpoints, and an occasional shepherd guiding his flock of sheep across the road.

The farther he drove from Baghdad, the quieter the world became. The cacophony of the city gave way to the rustle of wind through dry grass and the chirping of birds. He rolled down the window, letting the warm air wash over him. The scent of dust, diesel, and sunbaked earth filled his lungs—scents he hadn't realized he missed.

As he approached the outskirts of Balad Ruz, his heart began to pound. The village looked smaller than he remembered. The buildings were faded, the roads uneven, but the mosque still stood tall in the center, its minaret rising like a sentinel over the town. Children played barefoot in the streets, and old men sat in the shade of date palms, sipping tea and watching the world.

His mother greeted him at the gate of their family home with trembling arms and eyes that had waited too long to see her son. Her embrace was warm, but her frame had grown smaller, more fragile. They didn't speak at first. They didn't need to. A long hug was what they both needed. The silence between them was filled by years of longing and the unspoken grief of a family torn apart by war.

He had become accustomed to a completely different way of life, but for two weeks, Omar stayed in the village. The streets were narrower than he remembered. The houses on his street were more worn. But the people, his people, welcomed him with open hearts.

On the third day, word spread that Dr. Omar was offering free health check-ups in the old schoolhouse. By mid-morning, a line had formed outside the door—elderly men with canes, mothers holding babies, children with curious eyes. Inside, Omar set up a makeshift clinic with a folding table, a stethoscope, a blood pressure cuff, and a small box of donated medications.

"Doctor, my back has been hurting for months," said an old farmer, his hands calloused and stained with earth.

Omar smiled gently. "Let's take a look. Sit here, Uncle."

A young girl with a persistent cough sat quietly while her mother explained how they couldn't afford to see a doctor in the city. Omar listened to her lungs, gave her mother instructions, and handed her a small bottle of syrup.

Villagers brought him tea, dates, and flatbread. One woman insisted he take a jar of honey from her family's beehive. Another offered him a handwoven scarf. He accepted each gift with humility, overwhelmed by their generosity.

One afternoon, as he stepped outside to stretch his legs, he heard a familiar voice call. "Omar? Is that really you?"

He turned to see three men approaching. Older, broader, but unmistakable. It was Kareem, Hassan, and Majid, his childhood friends. They had played soccer in the dusty streets and fields, raced donkeys through the olive groves, and shared secrets under the stars.

"Kareem!" Omar laughed, embracing him. "You still have that crooked smile."

"And you still have that serious face," Kareem teased. "Even as a doctor!"

They sat under the shade of a fig tree, reminiscing about the past. Majid had become a teacher in the nearby town. Hassan ran a small shop. Kareem, who had once dreamed of becoming a pilot, now worked repairing farm equipment.

"You left, Omar," Hassan said, not with bitterness, but with quiet reflection. "You made it out. We always knew you would become more."

"I didn't forget," Omar replied. "I just needed time. But I'm here now, and I'll keep coming back."

They talked for hours, laughing over old mischiefs and mourning lost friends. Time had taken many things, but not their bond.

In the evenings, Omar would sit with his mother on the rooftop, where the stars shone as brightly as they had in his childhood. They talked about his father, about his laugh, his stubbornness, his dreams. They cried together, and they laughed, too. Time had softened the pain, but it had not erased it.

"I've forgiven them," Omar said one night, his voice barely above a whisper. "I had a lot of hate for the soldiers who took Baba's life."

His mother nodded. "So have I, my son. Carrying hate is too heavy."

The following morning, Omar's mom made Kahi Geymar for her son. The kitchen filled with the comforting aroma of butter and warm pastry as she carefully layered the dough, brushing each sheet with ghee before sliding it into the oven.

"I made you something, Omar," she said, her voice soft with affection. "Something I know you haven't had in a long time."

Omar looked up from the table, his eyes catching the golden, flaky pastry she placed before him. On top, she spooned a generous dollop of Geymar—a rich, velvety clotted cream that shimmered in the morning light. She drizzled it with date syrup, the deep amber liquid pooling slightly at the edges.

The first bite was like stepping into a memory. The crisp layers of the Kahi gave way to the cool, creamy sweetness of the Geymar, a contrast so perfect it made him pause. It was more than breakfast—it was comfort, tradition, and love, folded into one plate.

Omar's eyes closed and a smile filled his face, "Oh Momma, thank you."

Together they ate and sipped tea.

"Momma, I will be back sooner this time. You have my word," Omar said.

His mom gently placed her hand on his. "I am so proud of you, my son."

When it was time to leave, Omar felt a tug in his heart he hadn't expected. Iraq no longer felt like home, but it no longer felt like a stranger. As he boarded the plane to Cleveland, he made himself a quiet promise: he would return. Not just to see his mother, but to serve. To give back to the village that raised him.

This time, he would not wait so long. Once a year, at least—that was his vow.

28
WHAT'S HOME?

Jack had moved so many times in his life that the idea of "home" was more of a question than a place. As a kid, he had bounced between California and Texas like a pinball, ricocheting off the edges of family decisions and emergencies, job changes, and the unpredictable tides of life. He knew I-40 like an old friend—every rest stop, every roadside diner, every faded billboard that promised the world but delivered only a dusty parking lot and a tepid soda.

Some kids grew up with a backyard tree or a kitchen door they could measure their height against. Jack had mile markers.

He remembered the giant twin arrows in Arizona, once a bustling roadside stop filled with tourists snapping photos and browsing the gift shop. Over the years, the storefront emptied, the crowds disappeared, and all that remained were two massive, weather-worn arrows, faded yellow and red, cemented into the ground like relics from another time.

Then there was the leaning water tower in Groom, Texas. Every time he had passed it, he noticed something new: a fresh coat of paint, a new sign, or sometimes just the way the light hit it differently. It stood like a sentinel on the plains, marking time.

Jack had seen roadside attractions rise with fanfare, full of promise and novelty, only to slowly decay, claimed by rust, weeds, and silence. Some reopened briefly, like ghosts trying to relive their glory days, only to close again. Nature always won in the end.

These places became his landmarks, not just of geography, but of memory. There were no pencil marks to show Jack's growth, but these dusty towns marked his passage through time all the same.

Once Elena was by his side, the pattern of movement continued. The military sent them from East Coast to West Coast and everywhere in between. They lived in cities that barely slept and small towns that barely woke up. They moved with precision, like clockwork, packing and unpacking their lives into cardboard boxes labeled in black marker: Kitchen, Books, Jack's Tools, Elena's Office. Each new house was a temporary shelter, a place to sleep and eat and plan for the next move.

Even after military retirement, the pattern lingered. They chased opportunity, chased peace, chased something they couldn't quite name. Jack often found himself staring out the window of a new home, wondering if this was it, if this was finally home.

But what was home, really? A place? A feeling? A person?

Sometimes it felt like an imaginary word, like something people talked about in movies or wrote about in books. Close friends would share stories of growing up in the same place and returning home to start their families. It sounded like something out of a Hallmark movie to Jack.

For Jack, home had always been more fluid, more elusive. Home was Elena's laugh in the kitchen. Lying next to her at night, one arm holding her close. Listening to the girls play with dolls in their room. It was the sound of tires humming on the highway. It was the smell of desert rain and the sight of the Pacific Ocean after a long drive west.

He woke early one morning and wrote out the moves he had made, as far back as he could remember.

Sacramento, CA to Wellington, TX

Wellington, TX to Hollis, OK

Hollis, OK to Altus, OK

Altus, OK to Sacramento, CA

Sacramento, CA to Wellington, TX

Wellington, TX to Sacramento, CA

Sacramento, CA to Fort Sill, OK

Fort Sill, OK to Fort Bliss, TX

Fort Bliss, TX to Meinz, Germany

Meinz, Germany to Fort Carson, CO

Fort Carson, CO to Sacramento, CA

Sacramento, CA to Big Spring, TX

Big Spring, TX to Sacramento, CA

Sacramento, CA to Fort Campbell, KY

Fort Campbell, KY to Fort Hood, TX

Fort Hood, TX to Chillicothe, OH

Chillicothe, OH to Hillsboro, OH

Hillsboro, OH to Columbus, OH

Columbus, OH to Vallejo, CA

Vallejo, CA to Folsom, CA

Folsom, CA to Fort Worth, TX

Fort Worth, TX to Corte Madera, CA

Corte Madera, CA to Novato, CA

Novato, CA to Fort Worth, TX

Jack looked at the list. It didn't even include deployments or long stints at military schools. He knew there were more moves when he was a baby, from stories told by his sister and other family members. Looking at the list, he felt bewildered. Why so many moves? The military ones made sense, but all the rest ... Why was he always on the move, running from demons and what-ifs, or pursuing hopeful opportunities that offered different scenery?

The condo in Novato was nice, thought Jack.

As a kid, if given the choice, Jack would have stayed in Wellington without hesitation. It wasn't just a town—it was home to him. Even now, in the quiet corners of his memory, Wellington stood out like a warm light in a long hallway of moves and transitions. It was the one place that had never felt temporary. The streets were familiar, the faces recognizable, and the rhythm of life had matched the beat of his own heart.

He remembered the way the wind carried the scent of mesquite and dust, how the sun painted the fields in gold every evening, and how the dirt and gravel roads crunched beneath his feet as he raced toward nowhere in particular. The town was small, but it held everything that mattered—his grandma's house and the rodeo grounds where he played and dreamed of being a champion.

Wellington was consistent. In a life marked by change, it was the one place he could always return to in his mind and feel grounded. It was the backdrop of his childhood, the setting of his earliest friendships, and the place where he first began to understand who he was. Even now, years later, when the world felt too fast or too loud, Jack would close his eyes and picture those quiet streets, the wide Texas sky, and the freedom of being a kid.

Now, standing on the edge of another decision, Jack felt the pull of California again—a familiar tug in his chest, like the tide calling back a piece of driftwood. The state had partially raised him, released him, and welcomed him back more times than he could count. It was a place of beginnings and endings, of memories scattered across highways and coastlines. He had left pieces of himself there—some willingly, some not—and now he wondered if this time would be different. If this time it would stick.

"Would moving back to California be the right move?" he asked aloud, his voice barely louder than the breeze. The question hung in the air like dust in sunlight, suspended, shimmering, unresolved.

It had to be.

It felt right, but feeling right had become a strange norm—an instinct honed by years of movement, of chasing stability across state lines. Would this feel like a final stopping point? That was the better question. Could it be a place to forget that interstates existed that led to other lives, other versions of himself?

Moving had become etched into his DNA, a ritual repeated so often it felt like tradition. Pack the boxes. Tape them shut. Label which room they belonged to. Load things up. Say goodbye. Start over. Again and again. It was a part of military life, and honestly it had become how he coped, how he reset. But now, something had shifted.

A new figure had entered the mix—Father Time. Jack could feel him more clearly now, not just in the mirror, but in his bones. The hospital visits, the surgeries, the long recovery days spent staring at ceilings— all reminders that his body had been through wars both literal and personal. His knees ached in the mornings. His back protested every lift. His energy came in waves, and sometimes it didn't come at all.

He knew how much Elena loved California—not just for its beauty, but for the way it made her feel. The ocean air seemed to fill her with joy, and the mountains warmed her soul.

This had to be it, he thought. No more.

No more chasing the next place. No more pretending he had endless time to figure it out. This time, California wasn't just a destination— it was a quiet reckoning. A place to finally lay down the weight of wandering, to trade motion for meaning, and to stop chasing who he might become and simply live as who he was.

29
ONE MORE MOVE

The Fort Worth sun was rising fast by the time Jack loaded the last pieces of luggage into Elena's car and Jack's truck. The heat slowly danced off the pavement. It was unusually warm for a fall day. The neighborhood was still asleep, save for a few dogs barking down the street. Claire jumped around their legs, excited to be going on a new adventure. Elena stood by the front porch, arms crossed, watching the movers load the last of their furniture into the truck. Her eyes were hidden behind sunglasses, but Jack knew the look on her face. It was the same one she wore every time they left a place behind: part resolve, part grief, part anticipation.

They had done this too many times to count. But this time it felt different.

This time, they were going to what felt like home.

At least that's what Jack kept telling himself.

They didn't take the fastest route. Jack had insisted on a detour—one last visit to Wellington. With each visit, the town got smaller and smaller. Just a little piece of the Panhandle, where the wind never stopped blowing and the past never quite let go. Jack's mother and grandparents were buried there, in a small cemetery on the edge of town, shaded by scattered cottonwoods, bordered on one side by a stone wall and by rusted barbed wire on the other.

They arrived at the cemetery a little after noon. The sky was painted a deep blue, with white cottony clouds, and the air smelled of dry grass and freshly plowed fields. Jack walked slowly between the headstones,

Elena trailing a few steps behind. He knelt at his mother's grave, brushed away a few leaves, and then placed before the headstone a small bouquet of wildflowers he'd picked along the road.

"I thought I'd be back sooner," he whispered. "But you know how life goes."

Jack and Elena stayed for a while, not speaking much. Just being. Jack's thoughts drifted to the rodeo grounds. Before they left town, he drove Elena past the old arena. It was mostly abandoned now, the bleachers sagging and the gates rusted shut, but he could still hear the echoes of hooves and cheers.

"That's where I learned to ride," he said, pointing. "And where I rode my first bronc. I've been tossed in that dirt more times than I can remember."

Elena smiled. "I wish I could have seen you then."

"Oh girl, you would have fallen in love with my wild curls."

Elena laughed.

"Chute number one," he pointed. "That's where my buddy and I would round up a steer and get it ready to be ridden. We were little kids, living our daydreams one ride at a time."

The numbers on the chutes were hard to make out now, but Jack knew them by heart. They were a part of him. He walked around the arena and through the chutes, reliving each memory. He wanted to take part of the place with him, but he knew each piece of the arena needed to stay together. Stay here.

Afterward, they left Elena's car parked by the cemetery and made a lap around the town. The town square seemed smaller to Jack. He remembered running around, stopping at his great-uncle's barber shop, laughing and joking with the older gentlemen as they complained about the weather and gossiped.

The high school football field looked the same. Some new paint here and there, but still the home of the Rockets. On Friday nights in the fall, the place would be filled with people cheering and sharing larger-than-life stories of their own time running on the turf.

"It's funny," Jack said. "As a kid, I always figured I'd run on this football field with my friends. Wearing the red and white uniform. With each move back out here, I would hope and pray it would be the last. That we'd settle down."

Jack's words were soft, almost dreamlike. Elena gently touched his shoulder and slid her hand along his back.

From there it was back to the cemetery, and one more goodbye to his mom and grandparents. Then Elena followed Jack down County Road 1035 to 203. Jack pulled over, and Elena stopped behind him.

"I just needed one more look. One more feel of the red dirt through my hands."

She understood.

From 203 they got on 287 and headed northwest to Amarillo. Jack had a flashback of when his grandmother had taken him there for his first big rodeo event, when he was 10. He remembered the thrill of the crowd, the smell of popcorn and horses, the way the cowboys seemed larger than life. They drove past the old coliseum where it had all happened, where a little boy dreamed. It was still standing, though here, too, the paint had paled and the parking lot had grown cracked with weeds.

They didn't stay long. Just enough time for Jack to take a photo and stare at it for a few seconds. He could see that day in the picture, as if it were an old film playing.

"I know people drive through this landscape and think, how can anyone live here? Why move to this flat barren land? I get it, but for me, it's special. When I look across the horizon I see my life. My dreams. Some of my sorrows."

Jack's voice cracked, the emotions audible in each word.

"It's your history, right before your eyes," said Elena, her words spot-on.

It was Jack's history, right there, and he felt blessed to have it.

Before leaving Amarillo, Jack insisted they eat at the Big Texan. Elena knew all about the Big Texan, famous for its free 72-ounce steak challenge. Jack had shared stories of the place being a special treat when he was a kid. And they, too, had brought their girls here when they were little. Jack walked in and instinctually listened to his boots clopping on the wood floorboards. The sound reminded him of his first visit.

After their meal, Jack walked into the gift shop and purchased a little sticker of the outside view of the Big Texan. He knew this was most likely the last time he would visit.

They topped off their cars and headed back out onto I-40, passing Cadillac Ranch just out of town. The smell of the Lonestar Stockyards filled the air for miles. Then slowly the landscape changed from grasslands to high desert mesas and they were in New Mexico.

Their next stop was Santa Fe, a place Elena had always held close to her heart. The moment they pulled into town, the air seemed to change. It was thinner, cooler, laced with the scent of piñon smoke and desert sage. The adobe buildings glowed in soft shades of terracotta and rose, their rounded corners and wooden vigas casting long shadows in the late afternoon sun. It felt like stepping into a painting, one brushed with centuries of culture, color, and quiet magic.

They stayed at a small inn just off Canyon Road, where the walls were adorned with local art and the courtyard was shaded by cottonwoods. Claire curled up on the cool tile floor and watched hummingbirds flit between feeders.

During the day, they wandered through the historic plaza, where street musicians played Spanish guitar and native artisans displayed handcrafted jewelry on woven blankets. Elena tried on turquoise earrings while Jack admired the intricate silverwork of a Navajo belt buckle. They browsed galleries filled with clay pottery, oil landscapes, and abstract sculptures, each piece telling a story of the land and its people.

They lunched at a café tucked behind a stucco wall, where the tables were scattered beneath a canopy of grapevines. The green chili stew was rich and smoky, served with warm blue corn tortillas and a side of roasted squash. Hummingbirds zipped through the courtyard like tiny, jeweled rockets, pausing just long enough to hover near the blossoms before vanishing again.

On the second evening, they climbed to a rooftop patio above a wine bar, where the view stretched out over the low-slung city to the Sangre de Cristo Mountains, their peaks tinged with lavender and gold. The sky was a canvas of soft pastels, and the air carried the faint sound of wind chimes and distant laughter.

Elena swirled her glass of red wine and leaned back in her chair, eyes fixed on the horizon. "I could live here," she said, half-serious, her voice soft with wonder.

Jack nodded, taking in the view. "Me, too. But not now."

They sat in comfortable silence, the kind that only comes after years of shared roads and quiet understanding. The sun dipped behind the mountains, and the city lights began to twinkle below—warm, inviting, alive.

It was a place that felt like it had been waiting for them, even if only for a visit. They both knew this wasn't the destination. It was a beautiful pause. A breath before the final stretch.

The next day they left Sante Fe in the rearview mirror and took I-25 toward Albuquerque. Then it was back on the familiar I-40, passing through the beautiful rich landscape of western New Mexico and climbing into the high desert of Arizona. The road wound through mesas and pine forests until they reached Flagstaff, where they checked into a small inn near downtown and walked to dinner at a cozy bistro tucked between bookstores and coffee shops. Afterward, they strolled through the cool mountain air, hand in hand, listening to the quiet hum of the town winding down for the night.

Jack breathed deeply. "Smells like pine and possibility," he said.

Elena leaned into him. "You're getting poetic in your old age."

"Just wait until we hit the Sierra Nevada," he said with a grin.

The next morning, they left early, the sun rising behind them as they descended from the mountains. At Kingman, they turned north onto Highway 93, heading toward Las Vegas. The desert stretched out endlessly, a sea of sand and scrub. Elena rolled down her window and let the wind whip through her hair.

They didn't stop in Vegas long, just enough to refuel and grab lunch. The city shimmered in the heat, all neon and noise, and Jack was eager to get back to the quiet.

From there, they took Highway 95 north, following the edge of the Mojave. The landscape changed subtly, with more rock, more silence, and more sky. They pulled over near a dry wash where a small herd of wild donkeys grazed in the distance.

Elena lit up. "Look at them! They are so cute!"

Jack smiled. "You say that every time."

"And I mean it every time."

They watched the donkeys for a while, the only sounds the wind and an occasional bray. It was one of those moments that didn't need to be photographed or posted, just remembered. Captured permanently in their minds.

Back in the car, Jack called Elena, and they talked as they drove through the town of Tonopah. Jack pointed out his window. "That's the haunted clown motel," he said. "Want to crash there tonight?"

Elena laughed. "You can, and I'll see you at Elizabeth's place!"

As they made their way north along Highway 95, Jack and Elena pulled off north of Hawthorne and went down to Walker Lake, a shimmering expanse of blue nestled against the arid desert mountains. The water was quiet, the surface rippling gently under a pale afternoon sky, reflecting the sky and clouds like a memory floating on glass. The silence was almost sacred, just the soft whisper of wind and the occasional cry of a hawk circling overhead.

As they stretched their legs and took in the view, a small band of wild horses appeared down the shore, manes tousled by the wind, hooves kicking up dust as they moved with effortless grace. Their coats shimmered in the sun—chestnut, grey, and gold. Their presence felt like something out of a dream.

Elena stood still, captivated. "They look like they belong to another time," she whispered.

Jack nodded, watching the horses walk along the bank of the lake. It was a fleeting moment, but timeless. Another unexpected gift from the road.

"How majestic," Elena said. "They are so beautiful."

"Yes. They are."

They each sat on a rock, letting the stillness settle around them. The horses grazed and moved slowly, occasionally glancing toward them but never startled, as if they understood they were being admired. Jack appreciated how wild they were. Their freedom. The kid in him couldn't help but think about riding one, bareback, no saddle, just wind and speed and the open desert.

He chuckled softly at the thought. "You know, when I was 10, I would've sworn I could rope one and ride him through this amazing landscape."

Elena smiled, eyes still on the horses. "And now?"

"Now I just want to let them be. Enjoy the visual tale and let them stay wild."

They sat there for nearly a half hour, saying little, just watching. The sun dipped lower, casting long shadows across the lake. It was one of those rare, perfect exhales in life. Unplanned, unhurried, unforgettable.

Eventually, the horses moved on, disappearing into the distant brush and hills beyond the lake. Jack stood and stretched, brushing dust from his jeans.

"Ready?" he asked.

Elena nodded, but her eyes lingered on the horizon. "I'll remember this."

"So will I."

They walked back to the cars in silence, each of their hearts a little fuller, reminded once again why they had chosen to take this long journey west.

As the miles passed beneath the tires and the Sierra Nevada range loomed in the distance, Jack found himself drifting into memory. The last few years had been heavier than most, marked not just by moves and milestones but by moments that had nearly broken him. He remembered the accident vividly, the suddenness of it, the chaos, the pain. There were days he wasn't sure he'd walk again, let alone feel whole. The mental toll had been just as brutal: waves of anxiety, sleepless nights, and the quiet, creeping pall of depression. Then the aneurysm and emergency surgery in Cleveland had been a blur of bright lights, hushed voices, and the sterile chill of the hospital, followed by more pain and uncertainty.

There had been hospital stays, therapy sessions, and long, silent drives where he questioned everything. But through it all, Elena had been there, steady, patient, unshakable.

Now, as they drove west, the road unwinding like a ribbon of possibility, Jack felt the gravity of it all. He had lived a dozen lives, as soldier, husband, father, and survivor. The years of service with multiple deployments, the endless search for a job that would give him purpose, it had all shaped him, scarred him in some ways, but also strengthened him. Their daughters were grown now, carving out lives of their own. And for the first time in a long while, Jack didn't feel like he was running from something. No, he was moving toward something. A new chapter. A quieter one, hopefully, but no less meaningful. Life was fragile. He knew that now more than ever. And time with the people you love, that was the only thing that ever really mattered.

They crossed through Smith Valley, and just south of Carson City they started to climb into the Sierra Nevada. The beauty was breathtaking. Snow had already fallen on some of the higher peaks.

As they continued to climb, the air grew cooler and the trees taller. They skirted the edge of Lake Tahoe, where the water was a deep, impossible blue. Once they got on Highway 50, Jack pulled off onto Johnson Pass Road and drove up to the end. He parked and walked over to an overlook, and they stood in silence, taking it all in.

Jack took a deep breath and slowly exhaled. "This is where I'd come for peace," he said. "A couple days of nothing but me and nature."

"This," Elena said softly, "feels like coming home. I want to bottle this scent."

Jack nodded. "As a teenager I hiked all around these mountains. Up around Echo Lake and back into the Desolation Wilderness."

Jack held both his arms out wide, looked up to the sky and yelled, "I love you!" His voice carried across the mountainside and faded into the trees.

They followed Highway 50 west, winding through the mountains, passing old mining towns and alpine meadows. The South Fork of the American River rushed alongside them, the rushing water crashing over boulders and singing among the trees. The road narrowed and twisted, but Jack knew it well. He'd driven it as a teenager, as a young man, and now he was driving it again: older, wiser, and a little more tired.

As the sun was starting to set, they rolled into Camino, California. Jack's sister's house sat on a ridge among tall cedars. The scent of pine hung in the air. She came out to greet them, arms wide, tears in her eyes.

"You made it," she said, hugging them both.

"We always do," Jack replied.

That night, they sat on the back deck, watching the stars emerge one by one. The air was crisp, and the trees rustled in the breeze. Jack sipped a beer and looked out over the hills. They laughed over shared memories and talked about next steps.

"You two are welcome to stay with us as long as needed. I mean it." Jack's sister was adamant in her words and looked at Jack with a smile and loving eyes.

Jack nodded and raised his beer to her.

He thought about the journey, the miles, the memories, the moments. He thought about his mother and grandparents, about rodeos and wild horses and donkeys, about the winding roads that had brought him here.

And he thought about Elena, sitting beside him, her hand resting on his thigh.

"Do you think this is it?" he asked. "Home?"

She didn't answer right away. Just looked out at the stars.

"I think home is where we stop running," she said finally. "And where we start planting."

Jack smiled and paused before he spoke. "I don't know if I've been running from peace or it's been running from me, but right now, here, with you, I feel it. It's time we start planting."

30
CLAIRE

Before she was Claire, she was just another scrappy pup on the streets of Mexico City, dodging cars, scrounging for scraps, and sleeping wherever she could find a patch of shade. Life has been tough. She'd learned to be quick, quiet, and clever. But even the cleverest street dogs couldn't outrun illness. One day, she got sick, too sick to run, too sick to hide. That's when a kind stranger scooped her up and took her to a small veterinary clinic tucked between two taco stands.

The vet, a woman with gentle hands and a warm voice, treated her with care. She gave her medicine, food, and a soft blanket. Claire didn't know it then, but that visit would change her life. The vet worked with a rescue organization that helped street dogs find homes in the U.S. After a few weeks of recovery and filling out the necessary paperwork, Claire was placed with a foster family in San Jose, California. She had a yard, toys, and regular meals—luxuries she had only imagined and dreamt about before. *This is the life*, she thought. But something was still missing.

Then one day, she saw them.

Jack and Elena were walking through the park near her foster home, ambling toward her. Claire was lounging in the grass, pretending not to notice them, but she was watching closely. They looked kind. They laughed easily. They stopped and started talking to Linda, her foster mom. Elena knelt down and smiled at her, and Jack had that calm, steady energy that dogs just know. Claire tilted her head. *Are they here to see me? Could they be the ones? Should I play hard to get?* She had so many questions running through her little head.

Claire could hear Linda talking about her as the four of them walked around the park. Claire was curious about the discussions. The only thing she knew for sure was that Linda kept saying how sweet her pretty girl was. Though the words didn't make much sense, it was the childish tone that Claire could understand. That's when she knew they were talking about her.

"You should know that I am house-trained, and I have issues with squirrels," Claire said. She doubted they understood her, but she felt it necessary to share some details.

After about 15 minutes, Jack and Elena thanked Linda for her time. They each looked at Claire and smiled and said, "See you later, baby."

"Oh well. I guess they were here to just see Linda," Claire thought as she trotted back to her foster home. *"I should have said something about my twitch. It's a kind of beat I can't get out of my head!"* She plopped in her usual spot on a chair by the front door and dozed off.

A week later, her foster mom gave her some news: "Jack is coming to pick you up. Do you remember him?"

Claire looked at Linda. "What are you saying?" she asked. "Your tone is strange." She watched Linda pack up her toys and food. Then she saw her move her bed by the door.

"We must be going somewhere. Where? Where? Where?" she kept asking, but Linda wasn't listening.

Then there was a knock on the door. "I'll get it," Claire said over and over again, but the handle was out of her reach.

When Linda opened the door, Claire saw Jack. Then it clicked: *"He's taking me home."*

It was a strange time in the world, but Jack and Elena had decided it was the perfect time to open their hearts, and their home, to a rescue dog. And Claire, with her golden-blond coat and soulful eyes, had stolen theirs.

When Jack entered, Claire was nervous. She didn't know what to expect. But the moment he knelt down and whispered, "Hey there, sweetheart," something clicked. She wagged her tail cautiously, then leaned into his hand. It felt right.

The drive back was quiet. Claire curled up in her sleeping suite where it lay buckled in the passenger seat, occasionally glancing at Jack through the slits, as if to say, *Is this real? Am I really going home with you?*

From the moment she stepped into Jack and Elena's house, Claire became part of the family. She explored every room, sniffed every corner, and claimed the sunny spot by the living room window as her throne. Elena bought her a soft bed, but Claire preferred the couch, especially when the three of them would watch TV.

She was smart, affectionate, and a little bit sassy. She had a habit of storing snacks and hiding them in her bed. She barked at squirrels like it was her full-time job. And she had a dramatic flair for flopping onto her back with a sigh whenever she wanted belly rubs.

But more than anything, Claire brought joy. When life felt uncertain and heavy, she reminded Jack and Elena to laugh, to play, to go for walks just because the sun was shining. She was their silver lining.

She often wondered why they changed houses so often. But she didn't mind too much. She liked to travel, and most importantly, she was with her humans. That was all that mattered.

Years later, Claire was still by their side—older, wiser, but just as full of love. She had traveled with them across states, through deserts and mountains, always ready for the next adventure. As they settled into their new life back in California, Claire found the best sleeping spots in their new house. A soft chair by the front door with a blanket she had claimed. Curled up on the couch, content next to Jack and Elena.

She had found her forever home.

Anywhere Jack and Elena were.

31
HOME

For a little over a month, Jack and Elena stayed with his sister in Camino. It was close to orchards and wineries, and the quiet of the foothills gave them space to breathe, to rest, and to think. It was a soft landing after years of movement.

But Jack and Elena knew it was temporary. They were grateful— deeply so—for the warmth and generosity of Jack's sister, who had opened her home without hesitation. The days in Camino were peaceful, filled with quiet mornings, shared meals, and long talks on the back deck overlooking the orchards.

One evening, as the sun dipped behind the hills and the sky dissolved into a soft lavender glow, the three of them sat around the outdoor fire pit, sipping tea and watching the flames dance.

Jack's sister leaned back in her chair and looked at them both. "You know you're welcome to stay as long as you need," she said. "There's no rush."

Jack nodded, grateful. "We know. And we appreciate it more than we can say."

Elena smiled warmly. "It's been good for us. A chance to breathe."

"But," Jack added, glancing at Elena, "we need a place of our own. Somewhere to settle. Somewhere to begin again."

His sister nodded slowly, understanding. "You've always been moving, Jack. Even when you were younger. I think you've earned a place to land."

Elena reached for Jack's hand. "We're ready. Not just for a house—

but for a home. Something that's ours."

Jack's sister smiled, a little wistfully. "I hope you find it. And when you do, I hope it feels like peace."

They sat in silence for a while after that, the fire crackling between them. It was one of those rare, quiet moments where everything felt aligned—past, present, and future. Jack didn't know where their next stop would be, but he knew they were getting closer.

They found a rental property near Folsom Lake, tucked into the quiet neighborhoods of Granite Bay. It was modest, with a shaded backyard and enough space to feel like they weren't just passing through. The lake was close enough for evening walks, and the sunsets over the water became a ritual—one of those small, grounding joys that reminded them they were moving in the right direction.

Still, they kept looking.

One evening, just after dinner, Jack and Elena walked down to the lake, Claire trotting happily ahead of them. The air was cool, the sky streaked with soft pinks and oranges, and the water shimmered like glass. They found a quiet spot along the rocky shoreline and sat side by side, their legs stretched out, the stones warm beneath them from the day's sun.

Jack tossed a small pebble into the lake, watching the ripples spread. "You know," he said, "I didn't expect to like it here this much."

Elena smiled, pulling her sweater tighter around her shoulders. "Me neither. It's peaceful. The kind of quiet that feels earned."

He nodded. "There's something about the lake. It's not just beautiful—it's calming. Like it's been waiting for us."

"I love the way the light hits the water," Elena said softly. "And the trees. The way they frame everything. It feels like a painting."

Jack looked over at her, the fading light catching in her eyes. "Do you think we could stay here? Not just in this house, but in this area?"

"I think we could," she said. "I think we should."

They sat in silence for a while, listening to the gentle lapping of the water and the distant call of a bird settling in for the night. In that moment, surrounded by the quiet beauty of the lake and the soft rhythm of the evening, Jack felt something he hadn't felt in a long time—contentment. Not the fleeting kind, but the deep, rooted kind. The kind that whispered: *You're where you're supposed to be.*

It took a little over a year. A dozen open houses. Countless drives through neighborhoods, each trip filled with hope and hesitation. They'd walked through homes that were too modern, too cramped, too cold. There were a few near-misses—places that almost felt right, but not quite. And one heartbreak, when a deal fell through at the last minute, leaving them both deflated and wondering if they'd ever find a place that felt like theirs.

But then, they found it: a little bungalow near downtown Roseville, built in 1930, with a wide front porch that seemed to invite them in before they even reached the steps. The exterior was painted a soft, weathered sage green, with white trim and a front door that had clearly seen decades of hellos and goodbyes. The yard was modest but charming, with a few dormant rose bushes and a towering oak that cast long shadows across the lawn.

The moment they stepped inside, they knew.

The hardwood floors creaked just right beneath their feet—not in a way that felt old, but in a way that felt lived-in. The kind of creak that whispered stories.

The light poured in through the windows, golden and soft, catching the edges of the built-in shelves and an arched doorway that led into the dining room.

The rooms weren't large, but they were warm, cozy, and honest. There was a fireplace with a brick hearth, a small breakfast nook with a view of the backyard, and crown molding that had survived generations.

Jack stood in the living room, turning slowly, taking it all in. "It feels like it's been waiting for us," he said quietly.

Elena nodded, her eyes scanning the space. "It's not perfect," she said, "but it's real. It feels like a home. Like the kind of place you come back to, not just live in."

They walked through each room slowly, not saying much, just letting the house speak. In the back bedroom, the afternoon light filtered through gauzy curtains, casting soft patterns on the wall.

Jack looked at Elena. "I think this is it."

She smiled, her eyes misty. "I know it is."

They put in an offer on the house that night and closed the deal quickly. The timing was tight, but they managed to move in a week before Christmas. The first night, they sat on the floor of the living room, surrounded by boxes, sipping wine from plastic cups and watching Claire explore. Outside, the neighborhood twinkled with holiday lights. Inside, the house was quiet but full of promise.

Jack leaned back against the wall, looked around, and said, "We're home."

Elena reached for his hand. "Finally."

Jack looked at Elena, and she was already smiling.

"It feels right," she said.

It did.

They were home.

On Christmas Eve, they sat together on the porch, mugs of hot chocolate in hand, watching the neighborhood settle into a peaceful night. Occasionally they could hear children's laughter and their excited voices as they opened gifts. The air was crisp, and the stars above Roseville winked like old friends.

After a quiet moment, Elena smiled and said, "Do you remember our first real date? That tiny restaurant down the hill in Wakerheim, Germany?"

Jack chuckled. "How could I forget? We talked like we had known each other for years."

"You were nothing like the other Joes. Somehow you manage to still be a free spirit back then."

He nodded, eyes soft. "Back then, I couldn't have imagined this. Us. Everything we've been through."

"Me, neither," she said. "But I wouldn't trade it for anything."

Jack looked up and down the street and down at Claire, cuddled into a little ball on a blanket, the quiet hum of the streetlight breaking the silence. "It's not perfect," he said. "But it's ours."

Elena squeezed his hand. "And that's more than enough."

Jack looked around, then back at Elena.

"We made it," he said.

She nodded, leaning her head against his shoulder. "We really did."

And for the first time in a long time, Jack didn't feel like he was waiting for the next move. The next chapter. The next goodbye.

This was it.

Home.

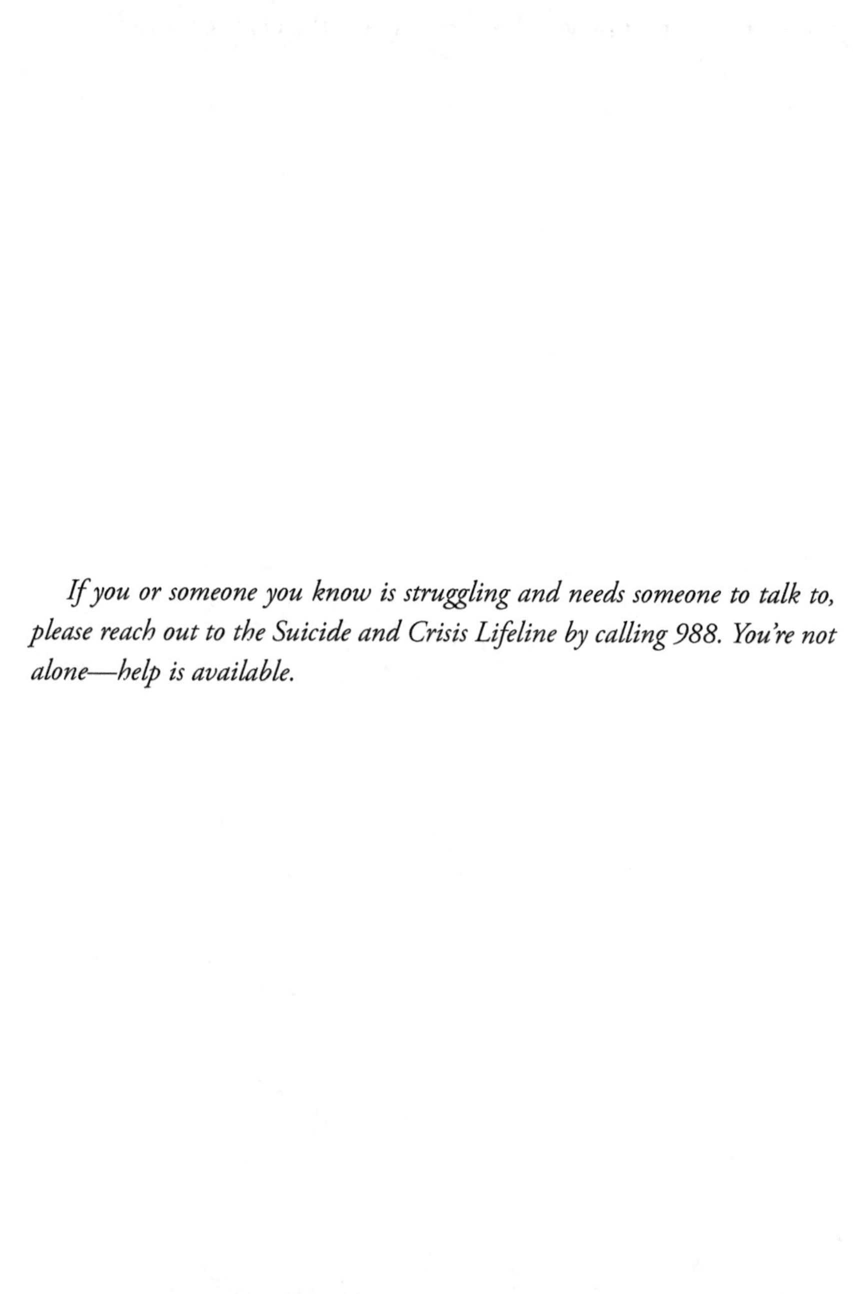

If you or someone you know is struggling and needs someone to talk to, please reach out to the Suicide and Crisis Lifeline by calling 988. You're not alone—help is available.

BRENDAN T. KELLY

Brendan T. Kelly classifies himself as a creative soul, whether it be storytelling, or making art in all of its lovely genres. Growing up, he split his time between Wellington, Texas and Sacramento, California; he'll tell you that he knew I-40 better than most truckers, at a very young age. Brendan served in the U.S. Army for 22 years, with duty stations around the world, to include multiple deployments. His writings are cultivated stories from the experiences he has had at all stages of his life.

He writes with a desire to help others, to share his stories, with hopes of helping people recognize that they are not alone, can get through difficult times, and not let the challenges or moment define them. Brendan shares his battles with PTSD and mental health in his writings, bringing the reader along for the ride, through the good and bad times.

Brendan completed his MBA with Columbia Southern, is a Lean Six Sigma Black Belt, Change Management Consultant, and holds other certifications. He has a passion for self-improvement and leadership. Brendan has been married to his beautiful wife for over 33 years. They have three amazing daughters (all grown now) and their dog Claire. Visit him at brendantkelly.com.

Absolute Love Publishing is an independent book publisher devoted to creating and publishing books that promote goodness in the world.

www.absolutelovepublishing.com